*The Shearing and other stories*

*The Corgi Series*  *Writing from Wales*

1. Dannie Abse, *Touch Wood*
2. Idris Davies, *A Carol for the Coalfield*
3. Mike Jenkins, *Laughter Tangled in Thorn*
4. *War*, an anthology edited by Dewi Roberts
5. Alun Richards, *Scandalous Thoughts*
6. Alun Lewis, *The Sentry*
7. Tony Curtis, *Considering Cassandra*
8. *Love*, an anthology edited by Dewi Roberts
9. Raymond Garlick, *The Delphic Voyage*
10. Rhys Davies, *Nightgown*
11. Sheenagh Pugh, *What If This Road*
12. *Places*, an anthology edited by Dewi Roberts
13. Leslie Norris, *Water*
14. T. H. Jones, *Lucky Jonah*
15. Paul Henry, *The Breath of Sleeping Boys*
16. *Work*, an anthology edited by Dewi Roberts
17. Harri Webb, *The Stone Face*
18. Geraint Goodwin, *The Shearing*
19. John Ormond, *Boundaries*
20. *Landscapes*, an anthology edited by Dewi Roberts
21. Glyn Jones, *The Common Path*
22. Gwyn Thomas, *Land! Land!*
23. Emyr Humphreys, *The Rigours of Inspection*
24. *Death*, an anthology edited by Dewi Roberts

*The Corgi Series*      *Writing from Wales*

# Geraint Goodwin
*The Shearing and other stories*

*Series editor*
**Meic Stephens**
Emeritus Professor of Welsh Writing in English
University of Glamorgan

Carreg Gwalch Cyf.

© Text: The estate of Geraint Goodwin

*All rights reserved. No part of this publication may be reproduced or transmitted, in any form or by any means, without permission.*

*ISBN: 0-86381-718-1*

*Cover design: Sian Parri*

*Carreg Gwalch Cyf. wishes to acknowledge the help of Martin Tinney Gallery, Cardiff (www.artwales.com) in supplying a slide of the artwork for the cover.*

*Logo design: Dylan Williams*

*First published in 2004 by Carreg Gwalch Cyf., 12 Iard yr Orsaf, Llanrwst, Wales LL26 0EH*
✆ *01492 642031*   ▤ *01492 641502*
✆ *books@carreg-gwalch.co.uk*
*website: www.carreg-gwalch.co.uk*

*Supported by an 'Arts for All' Lottery grant from the Arts Council of Wales*

We wish to thank the original publishers for their co-operation in producing this volume and for their kind permission to include material originally published by them.

# Contents

Introduction ..................................................6

The Flying Hours are Gone ..........................8

The Young Bull ...........................................17

The White Farm ..........................................29

Janet Ifans' Donkey ....................................43

The Shearing ...............................................70

For further reading ...................................108

# Geraint Goodwin (1903-41)

Geraint Goodwin was born on 1 May 1903 in Newtown, in the old county of Montgomeryshire, and educated at Towyn County School in Merioneth. After only four years there, he joined the staff of *The Montgomeryshire Express* and, shortly afterwards, left Wales for Fleet Street, working for *The Daily Sketch* as a reporter. In 1935, encouraged by Edward Garnett, he gave up journalism to become a full-time writer. By then he had contracted tuberculosis and spent several months in hospital and a sanatorium. Keenly interested in his Welsh roots, he decided to return to Wales in 1938, taking a cottage in the slate-village of Corris in Merioneth. His health continued to deteriorate, however, and with his wife and two children he moved to the market town of Montgomery. After another year in a sanatorium, he discharged himself and joined his family in their new home, where he died on 18 October 1941.

During his brief career as a writer, Geraint Goodwin wrote, besides *Conversations with George Moore* (1929), four novels and a collection of short stories. They are *Call Back Yesterday* (1934), *The Heyday in the Blood* (1936), *Watch for the Morning* (1938), *Come Michaelmas* (1939), and *The White Farm* (1937). All four novels and most of his stories are set in the Border country between Wales and England, and explore the differences between the squalid, anglicised town of 'Moreton' and the rural, Welsh-speaking parts of his native county, to which he was more attracted. Many of his characters are either strong-willed, passionate, fecund women or hapless, physically weak men, such as are also to be found in the work of D.H. Lawrence and Rhys Davies. Sexual rivalry is addressed in a forthright manner and he is not averse to tackling the more earthy aspects of human behaviour. Unlike Caradoc Evans, however, he portrays Welsh country people with sympathy, tenderness and humour, and their daily round in field and farmyard in authentic detail.

To the fifteen stories published in *The White Farm* were added another eight in *The Collected Stories of Geraint Goodwin* which appeared, under the editorship of Roland Mathias and Sam Adams, in 1976. Goodwin's novels had been very favourably received by the critics at the time of their first publication but that collection, now long out of print, together with the latter's monograph in the *Writers of Wales* series, drew attention to a short-story writer of remarkable gifts. This small selection of his stories in the Corgi series will go some way towards rekindling interest in an unjustly neglected writer.

# The Flying Hours are Gone

I remember everything; one cannot help memory. We come back after fifteen years and a great gulf divides us; we have changed and we look at the world, this world, as at a different place. We think that everything has changed with us and then we see a tree just as it had always been, and the old weir with a timber loose and the timber is still loose; an old gnarled branch, black and sodden, had been caught in the mill-race and it is still there!

This plantation – a planting we called it – seems just the same. It covers all the side of the mountain. It was fearful to walk into it; there was no sound to our footsteps and it was always dark. We liked to think – what did we think in those echoless depths – that somewhere always just beyond the reach of vision there were other shapes, moving like shadows, vague and phantasmal; like a dream that remains on the edge of memory, remote and unseizable. And there, too, we felt a strange, compelling presence, the presence of the wood, something primitive and elemental. How absurd it all seems now. The wood of course was like any other wood and with that lattice of branches shutting off the sun, with here and there a spike of light descending like a white lustrous rod, the carpet of pine-needles; why, no doubt it would seem strange.

I thought of all this as I sat there and I laughed at these young imaginings. All gone . . . ! That is the heresy of time that one can say with Elijah, 'Behold, there is nothing!'

I sat beside the favourite pool and remembered the great fish in its black depths. Perhaps they were still there. I remembered that intangible thrill as one slithered over the mossy stones to cast a fly under the alders, the whole being braced with a quickened consciousness of life. One heard the twenty tiny metallic tinkles of twenty streams breaking over the boulders and there would be just a flash, a sprung crescent of silver and . . . I subscribed to a fishing paper for a long time afterwards but as one of the Elizabethans had said, the flying hours are gone. There was no recapturing those early days. By and by I got bored with everything to do with fishing and really I can't tell you where I have put my rod.

People then predicted great things for me; I cannot for the life of me imagine that they had any cause. But my sincerity was a very real thing and it had the power of infecting others. They believed in me because I believed in myself. I was a law student at the National College of Wales at Aberystwyth, but this was but the outward guise that hid the inner aspect. At that time (how very *vieux jeu* it seems now), I believed in a new Wales; I was always speaking about our heritage and I would hint, in a sort of prophetic way, at our future. I must have got all my ideas from Renan, the all-enduring Celt, driven to the promontories of the world and nursing his proud spirit in solitude. I don't think it did me any harm; it is good for one to believe in something when one is young. How arid my degree course would have been without these, well, yes, dreams.

Still all this is neither here nor there. To continue with the story, I had put too big a strain on what St Francis called Brother Ass; the body did not rebel for there was no rebellion left; it collapsed. I came here, to that farm on the edge of the planting and I spent a winter there. Every morning I had half a pint of stout, a glass of warm milk straight from the cow and a raw egg, and then I had the same again in the evening. But I did not grow any fatter. I remember I used to weigh myself on the scales in the little station and chalk up my weight on the 'traffic regulations' on the wall. Good lord! perhaps they are there still. The horror of watching the little sliding racket . . . I always used to argue that the scales were wrong. I won't go into details but you know how one always looks into one's handkerchief after one has coughed and then one looks into the glass and sees one's jawbones sticking out and tries to arrange one's face differently; but they always stick out. And the despair that welled up in my heart!

I could not have gone through with it but for her. Of course there were times when she could not reach me, those times when the panic fear of death used to encompass me and one would go walking off into the mountains. One would stand still before a larch, all shriven in the winter, and say: 'There will be leaves next spring; a few months at most and the buds will burst out like little violent flames. I wonder if I shall ever see them.' And a collie all blown about by the wind would rush out of a byre, barking, and you would smell the cows and then the twilight would come and there seemed to be a strange and almost fearful light on the mountain where the last of the day remained. At such times the whole landscape would seem to be transformed into something strange and other-worldly.

All this I remember now but, as I have said, only as one remembers a dream. It may have happened, it *did* happen, but it remains just beyond the reaches of the mind: one rakes over the memory but one is only vouchsafed a glimpse like a familiar face one sees in the darkness.

Ah yes, but I remember all about the place, the old oak dresser in the kitchen (it was worth hundreds of pounds I used to tell them) and the brass harness above the fireplace and the blue tea-canister with a picture of the King on it and a picture of General Buller after some battle or another and of course, on the sewing machine in the corner, The Book, from whence issued, like a wraith, the grim colourless God of our fathers.

But these are only the external things. I can't for the life of me remember that something which is all there is to remember. I can't even recall what she looked like though I should surely know her again. She was tall and dark with violet eyes, yes they were violet or a peculiar shade of blue, and they really were the most expressive eyes I have ever seen. It made one sad to look into them – not really sad if you understand but one began to think about life in a vague kind of way. But as I say, I can never quite remember . . .

On the top of the hill was an old ring of piled-up stones. Half sunk in the ground and pockmarked with lichen, they reared their arrogant old heads as though defying time. Some said that this was really a 'castle', but they were more likely the remains of a druidic circle; and indeed to come up out of that wood by moonlight, to walk across the sward, was to become aware of something, some knowledge that one could never utter, that . . .

Well, we went up there for the last time. I was going away on the Monday, back to college, back to work. I was going to face up to the future again. How bright everything seemed. That hideous cloud had lifted at last. I felt like a small boy who has waited and waited for his birthday and then suddenly realizes after the months, the weeks, that it is the day after tomorrow!

I remember that she had put on her Sunday dress.

'What have you done that for?' I said.

'Only because I want to,' she answered sadly.

She was sitting on one of the stones, knees bent up, her head on her hands, looking out into the darkness. I suddenly realized that this was all she could do, all she could do to show how sorry she was that I was going. I felt very sad. I felt a sense of compassion that I had never known before nor ever was to know again. That poor little black dress that some dressmaker had run together in the market-town when her mother had died five years before.

She had done this for me, she loved me with all her soul, she had tended me through all the winter, she had seen me, like an arrogant young hawk begin to stretch his wings and venture forth ... and then life would settle down as before, settle down with its awful inevitability and encompass her. Yet she could say nothing.

'Ceri,' I said, 'Ceri ... '

I felt an ominous dread right down to the depths. I felt afraid of myself and of the future and of what the future might do for me. I buried my head on her lap and began to sob. They were the last scalding tears of youth.

'Help me to remember, Ceri, help me to

remember . . . ' I said and the words seemed to come from my heart.

She lifted my head between her hands.

But all this was long ago and you can see what might have happened. I had stopped dead on the brink of a chasm; I might have gone plunging down – where, whither? And now, long after, I know that I was right. I could not then have supported myself, I had not even begun a career. The most important thing in life, whatever the sentimentalists say, is to get a roof over one's head. Well, I have a roof over my head, though it is not a very big one, and I have never thought it necessary to marry.

I had taken my degree and had been called at one of the Inns of Court. I had forgotten to talk about a new Wales, for a Welshman in London has enough to live down without all that. I once thought of changing my name – something with a real good Anglo-Saxon flavour to it – but it was not easy. And if I could have changed my profession I would have done so, for the law is one of the most bourgeois of callings and there are more kicks than ha'pence for the son of a road-mender even though his father carried Thucydides (in the original) in the backside of his corduroys. After four years I could point to an acquittal at Nottingham Assizes (under the Poor Persons Act) and a few words of commendation from the judge and that was about all.

And so I drifted into journalism – after all it is only crossing the street – and became leader-writer for a good nonconformist paper and was able to spread myself out on disarmament, free speech and the right of small nations, and all those things which I had at heart. Some day, I said, when I had enough capital, I would go back to the law . . . but perhaps if I went back to the law I would say that some day I would go back to journalism . . .

And once a year I go back to Wales for my summer holidays, but it is never quite the same; one can never recall the past for there is always that gulf, as wide as – how wide? – why as wide as Time!

I can see from where I stand the old stones on the hillside and just the top of the house with its curl of smoke climbing over the trees, I can smell the peat, that smell which *is* the mountains to us who have been bred there. I can see a man trimming the hedge on the far end of the bye-take; it must be her husband. I can hear the dog barking and the cheep-cheep of the young turkeys and someone stepping across the cobbled yard and then the slamming of a door and then a child crying . . . I will go up and see her, I say. She would be glad to welcome me, I know, and I can even picture myself handing round coppers to the children and perhaps the best teapot will come down and the canister with the King's picture on it.

I had half opened the gate in the meadow; I watched the wind blow it shut again. And I was on the outside, standing with the present and the future. And beyond was the past, but a past that had not stood still. Where it had gone to I did not know.

# The Young Bull

She heard his horse clip-clopping into the yard and methodically dropped the kettle a rung on the spit. Then she stove her foot into the smouldering ashes, sending a little cloud of white dust into the room. She did it with a sullen defiance as though the fire were thwarting her, then moved back on to the settle and took up her knitting. She had a heavy, sullen way with her as though she were only half awake. Her eyes were heavy-lidded, her lips large and sensual and her body heavy and broad-hipped and slow in movement though she was well shaped. There had been no quiet in the house since she had come there. She was 'quert', they said. Also she was lazy. She had never settled down.

'A few young 'uns would ha' made a mort o' difference,' they said.

But there were no children though they had been married three years. Cae-bwgan, half timbered, half in Wales and half out of it, half pasture and half straggling off in a brown crust on to the Wimberry Hill, stood there above the coloured fields, sombre as a gibbet. It stood there in that eerie upland, breasting the fresh winds that came from the Welsh mountains, winds that rustled and groaned among the elms before spending themselves on the broad coloured valley of the Severn; Cae-bwgan (the goblin's field), perched between earth and heaven, a place between two worlds.

He was tall and loose limbed, moving with a strange easiness for the country. His hair was long and jet black and curled at the edges, and his eyes, deep set, were steel blue and always strangely menacing. The first thing you saw of him were the eyes and that peculiar colourless gaze. He had got into the habit of looking at the floor when he spoke because it made people uneasy to see him face to face. People called him 'Jack-look-down'; most often he was just Jack Caebwgan. No one had ever seen him angry.

There were strange stories told of him but as he came from over Clun way no one ever knew for certain. And he was the best farmer for miles around. Cae-bwgan had never seen the like before; it had put the valley farms to shame.

He came into the house with that strange easy slouch as though he had come through the wall. He still carried his crop and the green rimmed bowler which he wore for the auction was struck over his eyes.

His wife did not raise her eyes. She spoke from her knitting.

'How'd they do?'

'Fourteen and half.' His voice for so big a man was quiet and low-pitched. He could sound it, within its compass, as he liked.

'Top . . . ?'

'Aye, o' course. Me and Crogbren. "Them's Kerry Hills," they said – "best in Flock Book".'

'You'm proud o' yourself maybe,' she sneered.

That strange sense of strife that had broken them up was there. They were battling one against the other. There had been no peace in the house since he had brought her there. But she could never reach him, provoke him how she would. They were like two people fumbling in the dark and reaching out for one another. He would seldom answer her more than 'No-o' or 'Aye' or 'that's enough now' or 'let well alone'; it was like butting the wind. She had kept herself from him in the agony of her spirit. But he would not break. He had merely said:

''Appen I'm a gelding,' in a monotone. Then he laughed his low laugh. 'Ony you'm always a mare. And,' – with the first suggestion of a threat, 'ony dunna go breaking down any fences.'

She was a poor wife to him. He had not minded. His pride was in himself. And he had come back from the auction knowing that his fleeces, hill or no hill, had been coupled in the top price.

'You'm like a dog with two tails – dunna know which to wag,' she said, slamming down the dish of tea. She was getting his meal out of the range. It was a stew, all spoilt, the meat stringy, the lukewarm gravy floating on the top in little puddles of grease.

'Aye, that's right,' he said. 'A dog a comin' 'ome to his vomit. Take it away.'

She stood there, sullen, fuming.

'Take it away,' he said dropping his voice. 'Bring cheese. I'm too young for soddin' yet.'

She went to the dairy, why she did not know. She knew that she had to go. She returned with the cheese, bared almost to the rind. He went on with the meal in silence. Before him, stuck up between cup and jug, was a copy of the local paper which shielded her from him. It was as if she were not there.

'Is there anything you mind of but the Kerry Hills and the auld bull,' she said after a while. 'You'm not know if I was clemmed.'

'You inna clemmed,' he said, not raising his head. 'You'm line your side, come what may.' He held the saucer in his hand and blew over the tea.

'A woman inna all that struck on vishals,' she said, a strange note in her voice.

'Oh aye?' He looked up quizzingly. 'You'm tire in your own time then,' he said. His face was motionless, statuesque. He answered because he had to; there was no life in his voice.

'I inna a old hen to be trod as whens when.'

'Oh aye.' There was a sneer in his voice, in his thin, sardonic lips turned up in derision.

The woman jumped up from the settle, a red flush spreading down her neck; her eyes narrowed, her face drawn and malignant under her mounting colour.

"Appen I'd find my price,' she said. She flung the words at him in challenge, standing there on the brink of frenzy.

'Aye: 'appen! At a Dutch awkshun. Thee't sell theeself in the doin'.'

She stood facing him across the table, breathless, glaring.

"Appen I have . . . '

There was no sound but the heavy tick-tock of the grandfather clock, the clatter of the chain. Outside the windless heat, the nimbus of the brown earth; far away the thin smudge of hills like a blue daub on the skyline. The earth seemed to quiver in the heat, stream up like a mirage in the dead air. The whole of the world had been struck silent as though by the hand of death.

He got up from his chair. There was still the thin derisive curl in his lips.

"Appen thee hast. Pity thee't not raddled, then I'd know.' He turned to face her and she shrank involuntarily under the pale eyes. 'But if thee'st trailed round about here he'll get a charge of six-shot in his arse.' He jerked his thumb up to the rafters where his double-barrel hung.

He reached for his hat and drew himself up in that strange animal movement from the hips. At the door he said:

'Not for thy sake . . . for mine!'

She watched him turn into the farmyard. He had gone beyond her again, not into the farmyard but into his own world, that strange, spaceless, quiet world where he had his own being. And she was left contactless, revolving round her own axis, beyond the orbit of this larger light that she guessed at but could not enter. And she was left with that sense of frustration which welled up in her like a flood. It was death itself.

He had gone down to water the cattle. The duck pond beyond the wainhouse had dried up leaving its baked, cracked bottom like a festering sore. He had to take them to the brook at the bottom of the meadow. And first of all to go was the bull. It was the bull he had gone to now, unlatching the door of the shippen and patting its moist flank, running his hands down the glistening fetlocks and feeling, in the contact of touch, the beast's grand strength work within him like yeast, filling his belly with returning strength as a pond fills after rain. Then he would feel sure and complete again, some knot in his belly would unravel itself, and he would feel the warmth spread upwards, dripping through his fingers. His pride in the bull was a small thing beside it.

'Border Brigand' he had bought as a yearling. He had thrown it then, with his own hands, in a sudden exultant moment in the fields. It was on the stud book, was the best Hereford in that part of the Border, massive, with its grand arrogant head, its huge brisket, its sleek, gleaming coat; it stood there triumphant, immovable.

There was a strange sympathy between them. He alone could handle it; with him the beast was as docile as a lamb. He never used the pole; he never would use the pole. He was its master.

He unloosened it from the stall. The beast had chafed in the heat; there was foam on its flanks. He whisked it away with his hand and then led the animal into the yard. But he was not sure of himself; the contact between them was broken.

Then it was that the bull struck its short legs into the earth, bringing the massive body up with a jerk. Up went his head. At that moment the man knew that he was doomed. That instinctive, knowledgeless thing that caught him in the belly, bracing his body like a taut string, every sense quickened to an unbearable perception. And down his back, like a douch, went a sudden coldness bringing order out of chaos. He was like an animal with its ruff up. It was to be a fight to the death. He *knew*, as he backed away, never once letting his eyes move from the malignant glare of the bull, those eyes smouldering in the immense square front that faced him, all that there was to do. He had taken in the position without as much as a glance round. He slithered back on his soles ready to poise for a spring;. his limbs seemed to have dissolved about him into a unity. He took on the ageless crouch of the hunter who, thousands of years before, had made those barrows on the hillside. And, conscious of death, he exulted. He had gone beyond feeling.

On either side and behind him were the barns, forming three sides of a square. Towards this he was being backed, slowly, inevitably. He would be backed until he reached the wall and then savaged – this he knew. The fourth side was the open pasture, the neck of the yard half cluttered up with a wagonette. He dare not risk trying it, the two jumps, one on to the shafthead and then the other into the wagon itself. He dare not risk a scamper into the open pasture for there he would be run down with all the momentum of the great beast's charge. Within the yard, by its very lack of space, the bull moved uneasily and at walking pace.

Back and back he went. Then he felt the wall, the bricks hot on his outstretched hands. He picked up a pikel and held it at the present. The bull came on, tossing his head like a curvetting horse, before that last dreadful toss that was to hurl him through the air. Then he stove the pikel at the lowered head with all his might. He felt his body jar with the impact, down to his very toes. The steel prongs had penetrated to the great bone of the forehead and shivered on the haft. But it had brought the bull up momentarily. He slithered along for a spade – moved into the open. And then, with a sudden quick little trot, the bull was on him. He was down. He felt the hot breath on him, the saliva dropping, the great flapping dewlap over him, and with a final dreadful effort held on to consciousness. He felt the beast's horn pierce his breeches and slide along his ribs and then, with a wrench, his shirt and waistcoat fly from him. The bull had missed; it went curvetting about the yard, its horns festooned and shaken in fury. The next toss would do him.

Then it was he saw his wife. She had rushed across the open end of the yard on to the shafts of the wagonette. He saw her raise her skirt and tear off her red flannel petticoat. She was standing there on the shafthead, hallooing and shouting and waving her petticoat.

Slowly the bull pivoted, head lowered, taking in this new adversary.

'Get in; get in, you fule,' he shouted. His throat was dry. She would be whisked off those shafts like a bobbin.

She stood there defiant, her body poised there like a figure-head.

He scrambled to his feet, white with fury.

'Blast thee, woman. Lep back.'

'I wonna.' She tossed her head back. 'Thee run – if thee'st legs left.'

Again the bull turned. The naked man edging to

the wall, the screeching woman with the flapping petticoat, had fuddled it. The man bellowed, waved his hands, the woman shrieked and made to come off the shafthead. It was like some fantastic auction.

And then the bull settled it as between them. Suddenly his tail went up; he was away at the flapping petticoat.

The woman drew herself back to the wagonside, the bull passing her within inches, taking the petticoat on his horns and stumbling over the shafts. His great form reared and heaved and then stumbled and he was rolling on the meadow.

'Lep back. Lep back,' the man shouted. There were seconds to spare. And then in a quick run he was across the yard, had leapt on to the shafthead and struck her across the mouth, tumbling her back into the body of the wagon, he falling beside her with the force of the blow.

'That's for them as dunna answer.' He wiped the blood off his hand. His face, pale as death itself, was twisted in rage, the eyes flaming in the baneful red-rust light of the possessed; his hands, knotting and unknotting themselves like sprung joints, felt for her in his fury. He would have killed her. Then seeing her lying there, spread voluptuously on the straw, her heavy round breasts bursting the broken corsage like a dammed up stream, dead stagnant water bursting into life, her dress torn from her, his fury moved towards it like a licking flame shifted in the wind, leaping clean and solitary from the blue core at its centre.

"Appen we got to stay here now a bit – all night maybe,' he said through his teeth. He was breathless, exultant.

"Appen we dunna.' But she was not taunting him. She had probed him to the quick, to the life of him. Within her voice, as within her womb, was the triumph that moved her, a triumph that had come to her as surely as light, breaking up the hard knot of her mind, destroying reason, loosening her limbs into warmth and softness. Out of time it had come to her, working within her. She felt her joints dissolve within her and her belly gnaw at her. She felt as though she were being wafted up and carried away, beyond space, beyond time. She was drowsy with her desire.

She lay back on the straw seeing him standing above her. She saw him there with his pale, lithe body and his small hips and the thin sheen of hair like a cloud on his white body. She lay there and saw him, only him, and beyond him the sky, lightless, all-present; saw him as she had never seen him before, remote and pure in his singleness. He burnt before her like a flame.

And then suddenly like a fire smouldering blown into life, her desire blew into flame, searing, remorseless.

"Appen I dunna,' she said, tearing off her dress and hurling it at him, eyes ablaze, her body sprung with life. "Appen night wonna find us here.'

"Appen it does then.' Very quietly he felt for her, surely and quietly.

# The White Farm

He walked on to the little veranda and sniffed the morning breeze. It had become a rite now – on these days of holiday – the clear air off the sea, off the mountains, always seemed better in the early morning. But this morning it really was good, he thought. Inland, there was the clear-cut freshness of the mountainside, the fields all marked out and clear in their colours, and just a circle of mist, like a frill of steam, around the summits.

He took two or three deep breaths and heaved audibly. He was a big man, with a heavy aggressive jaw, his face very brown, and his brow, which reached up through the thin hair, blistered with sun and the salt water. His eyes were blue and sure and faintly contemptuous, and his hands large and clumsy.

He stood there on the little veranda, leaning against the door and watching his wife, very small and trim, shaking her dark hair back as she busied herself with the oil cooker, a white apron about her, and the little waist tied with a large bow. The small delicate movements of her, the large anxious eyes for ever fearful, always moved him.

He went over to her and put his big hands on her shoulders.

'What about today?' he said briefly.

She did not look up at him: instead, she slipped

free and went on with the cooking. They were up late and she was not quite herself.

'Where?' she asked over her shoulder.

'Pant what-you-call it,' he said, peeved. '*You* know.'

'If *you* like,' she said in the same matter-of-fact tone.

'If you like,' he went on. His heavy face went childish in his sulk. But he was going to humour her. He felt that he owed her something.

'But you've got the game!' she said, turning to him.

'That can wait,' he replied in the same peremptory way. 'They're nobody, anyhow,' he explained.

'But you promised,' she insisted.

'Did I? I said that I *might* make up a foursome.'

'Oh,' she said. 'That's different.'

'After all,' he went on magnanimously, 'I've got a wife.'

She did not answer, but turned to the stove again with a little shrug.

'It's not much fun for you . . . I know,' he said. He caught her by the shoulders again. 'My pretty one!'

She bowed her head on her breasts like a drooping bird. He felt uncomfortable, the words muddling him.

'My little one,' he said again in the same

tentative way. He squeezed her shoulders until she winced.

'Oh, leave me alone!' she cried out.

He went out on the veranda again. Perhaps, after all, it was his fault. But then, he told himself, they were on holiday, and after all a man was a man. But he was worried all the same. And yet things could be different. If only he had a square deal. That was the phrase always on his lips – a square deal. He wanted to know where he was – and where the other person was. Then they could get down to things. That had been the secret of his success – and he had been successful. He was hard, as he said, but always fair. Up North, he would explain, they were made like that.

But had he had a square deal, now, in the ever-present, from his wife? He wondered – he had begun to wonder more and more. He did not like to think that he had not – but he wondered. And now, at the end of a year of marriage, they were farther apart than at the beginning. They were not drifting apart so much as they *were* apart. And was it his fault? It was not that they had ever been together – her little world was like herself, so small and tender and wisp-like: for ever proof against his loud and obvious heartiness. It was like hammering on a closed door and blustering on the step: and there, beyond, was the quiet and the mystery.

And yet she loved him – there was no doubt about that. He had swept her off her feet and she had never found them again: the heavy aggressive sense of him, the I-am-what-I-am triumphant had, at first, bewildered and then captivated her. He was not sure how it had all come about, but he guessed it. And he continued to play his trump card – his only card – in the hope that things would right themselves. But it was up to him to give the lead – he felt that it would always be up to him to give the lead.

'Feeling better?' he said, when he went in. He gathered her in his arms but she turned her head away. Then he lifted up her chin. He knew how to humour her in his clumsy way.

'We'll be off in no time,' he said unctuously.

He went out into the sand-swept garden, with its line of sea thistles tossing, and tore the tarpaulin off the big saloon car. Then he began to tinker about with the engine, and then went round with a duster like an old maid dusting.

Within an hour they had started. He knew that it had to be done sometime – this journey to her father's people up in the mountains. The Welsh were funny people – they got something out of it, this journey to the old folks at home, even if the home were a hovel. And as they all had a home somewhere, they would all have to go back to it. Well – if it amused them! But the old man – he was a wealthy London-Welsh draper – was more Welsh than she was, and he seemed to care very little, for he spent his time at the bowling tournament at Eastbourne. A funny lot!

They had climbed beyond the little village but stopped once on the road to look back on it. In the summer sun it had come alight – just like a lot of broken china cups thrown on the shingle, and beyond it the blue fringe of sea running off into a haze. But that was the old village, with its one straight street and its white houses. Joined on it, like a fungus on an old bole, was the new part, with its modern red-tiled bungalows with their cream stucco sides. Beyond again was the golf links which reached right down to the sand-hills, blown up in a bulwark against the tides, the clumps of rushes white in the sun like scrubbed hair. The moist sour-green earth spread down to the *morfa* (the marsh) which lay inland. The land was all green, with the light burnt crust of sand as a ridge, and the washed smudge of sea and sky stretching into the distance – the whole stretch of Cardigan Bay cupped within its two arms, far in the south, far in the north.

'There they go,' he said, tracing his finger through the window.

She had sat huddled in the front seat, her mind gone off.

'That's them,' he said again, breaking into the quiet. 'That's old Wilkie – over there on the fifth tee. There now – he's driving.'

33

He looked at his wife sideways, the little core of resentment in him hardening.

'You're not going to get all het up again?' he asked.

'Why – of course not.'

'I said, that's old Wilkie.'

'Well! I saw.'

'That's about all,' he said, slipping into gear. It was not worth troubling about. But his friends were her friends.

'A bit bleak,' he said, after a while. They had left the main road and the lane went off over the gently swelling mountain, two parallel ruts sluiced with storm water which lay around in pools. Sometimes the track was half cluttered up with shale, sometimes the surface was worn through to the bare rock. Around about, the mountains rolled up in a gentle sweep with the mist lifting above them. Now and again there was a house, with the few wind-blown firs about it as shelter, its white, wet sides shining in the sun, and the bare yard with a white-eyed dog skulking, and the waddling geese.

'Oh, John,' she begged. 'Do stop.'

He braked hard, with a faint smile of amusement at her urgency. He liked doing this for her. She got out of the car and ran off through the wet heather and stood up on a mound, her breast heaving.

'Better now,' she said, as she took her place. Her

eyes were alight and dancing, and her lips wide open. He felt the load come off him. She excited him in the old way, so light and fresh in her young beauty, the poise and delight of her and the light in her face. She was something to be desired, as he first desired her – would always desire her. The rest was not there – had not happened.

He put his arm round her shoulder and crushed her to him.

'Not now,' she said, slipping free.

'Right,' he said, his mind reaching out at an infinite promise. 'A bargain!'

They had come to the brow of the last hill. Below them the road dropped into a *cwm*. A torrent tumbled over the mountain into it, swilling through the heather, leaping down into a spume of silver. And there, below them, was the house, standing out of the earth, with its upblown smoke curling up to them, and the pandemonium of barking dogs and the geese shrieking. It had all suddenly come to life.

A man was on the little trellis bridge, shouting. The dogs running up and down the track cowered down on their bellies and crawled back to him.

'*Uffern dân! Hei! Siân, Meg . . .* ' he shouted.

'That's uncle,' she said, the words strung in her excitement. 'He won't know me: he won't know me. Now for fun!'

The old man came up to the car as it stopped.

He had a round, full face, red with the weather, a grey fringe to it. It seemed hewn out in its angularity, and yet there was a light in it – a hardly distinguishable, distant gleam. And yet that was the face. The eyes were very blue and steadfast, and there seemed no end to them in their distance. He seemed always to be calling himself back as he spoke.

'The dogs will be barking,' he explained. 'Do not you mind them.'

He picked his words with great deliberation. But they were not sure whether he had seen them – his gently roving eyes had gone off again into the distance.

'*Dewch yma Sian!*' he shouted in a sudden roar. An old black sheepdog in the pack had gone slinking up for a furtive snap. Now she dropped on her paws and rolled her eyes up, her old head shaking in ecstasy. '*Beth sydd arno chi fach?*' he went on, sounding his voice as the old head rocked.

'She just come,' he went on. 'Her mister *wedi marw* – die, how you say? No teeth . . . see?' He opened her jaws.

'She obeys you?' said the husband.

'Oh yess,' he explained. 'You know how? I tell you. You get a bit of cheese, see, and put it under your arm. Then after long time you give it her. Never go after! A bitch, see – a bitch like that.'

'Wants a master,' said the husband, helping him out.

'Oh – I won't say.' He put up his hands with mock horror. The laughter filled his face like a brimming jug.

'Don't tell lies,' the woman said in Welsh, laughing outright.

The old man never moved, but he turned his eyes on her, as though bringing them out of the distance.

'*Cymraes?*' (A little Welsh girl?) he said in the same even voice.

'A Japanese *really!*'

'Tut, tut!'

The young man stood and watched his wife in wonder. The tilted face, impenitent, and the laughing eyes. She went bubbling on like a spring. The two went on in their cross-talk, the old man, out of deference to him, still labouring in English.

'I'll be going,' he said. He got out his rod and flung his basket over his shoulders. 'I'll follow the brook up,' he added in parting. 'Don't worry.'

The old man watched him go, his face hardening. It was not polite. And yet his going had eased it as between them. It was as if a shadow had lifted.

'Softie! Yr hen softie! I'm Dilys,' she said.

'Dilys! Wili's Dilys?'

She burst out laughing.

'You are a funny one.' He caught her by the arm and led her in.

'Well, well.' He said no more, his face beaming.

Beside the old hearth he said casually: 'Take your seat.' She belonged. The hard-reached deference had gone out of his voice. He gave the peat fire a stir with the poker and moved the kettle across the spit.

'Well, well,' he said again. He spoke in Welsh now, his voice dropping to the homely familiar note.

'*Mam*,' he called. '*Mam*.'

The old woman came in, her thin spindle body bent across, an old shawl over her shoulders. Her eyes were very quick and bright in the old worn face – only her eyes, thin and bright, for ever hovering.

'Here she is,' he said.

The old woman shuffled across and peered at her. '*Fach*,' she said, putting her arms around her. 'Oh, the little dear.'

She reached her feet into the fender and leaned back into the old horsehair chair. The worn old house possessed her – the brass harness round about, the old dresser with its line on line of blue china plate, the rich earth smell of the peat. That fire had never been out for two hundred years, her father had always told her. And here it was! And all around, through the little tight shut windows, was the moist green of the mountain, reaching up like a shelf, and the distant rumble of the brook.

*Pant-y-Pistyll* – the Hollow of the Spring. Always the drifting mist, for ever lifting, and the noise of the water, the sharp high tinkle to the deep, harsh earth-flooded roar of the winter: the green earth, the smell of peat and the high blue crust of the mountain – that was her home, her father's home, and that was where she belonged. She let it all possess her, gave herself up to it, as to a lover. She had gone away from herself, far, far away. Now she was – only now she was: never before, perhaps never again, but now she was.

'Oh, *Nain*' (grandmother), she said. She threw her arms around the old woman and bent her head in the old shawl.

'There, there,' said the old woman, brushing back her hair with her old withered hands. She pressed her to her old breasts and crooned to her as to a child, taking the deep, breaking sobs to herself.

'The old *hiraeth*' (longing), she said to her son, standing beside them. The old mother waved him away. He went out into the yard.

When she came out again, her eyes red and fresh, he was standing there, just as she had first seen him. Beyond him, across the brook, was the little chapel, small and grey and silent, and around it was the little wall of piled stones, lurching up against the weather, a tiny yellow sprinkle of stonecrop spilt across it. Tied on the gate was a little tin offertory box that rattled in the wind. Beyond, the grey stone slabs stood up on end among the lank grass. That and the farm were the only buildings for miles: beyond the land ran off into the mountain.

'It's time your father came back,' he said.

She bowed her head.

'Never mind,' he said gaily. 'Plenty of time. You tell him we are still here.'

They had walked beyond the little graveyard to the lush hay-field. At the bottom was the river running down the valley in a brown fresh: the little brook leapt to meet it.

'Where is Morlais?' she asked.

He pointed over the sheep-walk on the mountain. 'He can't go far now.' He pointed to his hip. 'A horse kick him. Pity – ay, indeed. A strong chap too.'

He shook his head, destroying the memory of his son's hurt.

'You were only little things – last time,' he said. 'Hair down your back.'

'Fifteen years,' she said.

'Sure to be.' He looked into the distance and nodded.

'You made a house to play,' he said, 'out of the old wall.'

'Down there,' he went on, pointing.

She followed his finger. The old stones were still trailed about the field.

40

'Awful mess that house,' he said, wagging his head. 'So *serious*, you two.'

'Fun!' she said savagely. She could not see through the cloud of tears. She twisted and untwisted her glove and turned her head away.

'You'll be waiting for Morlais?' he asked.

'No!' she cried out.

'Pity. He'll be that sorry.'

'We must get back,' she said, a note of terror in her voice. She ran into the field in her anguish, the wet grass to her waist. The old man followed her.

'Take time: take time,' he called gently. 'No *great* hurry.'

He went on up the river calling, leaving her alone. She stood there beside the water. Years ago she and Morlais had gone off to look for its source. They never found it: they never would find it. It had no beginning as it had no end. She remembered and yet she could not remember. It was so long ago.

The water went by in a fresh, lightless and gleaming, and then beyond her through the gorge which led out to the sea; it went by her, strangely dark and gleaming, with the tufts of foam swilling down its centre in a long white line. And all above it were the hills, heavy and brooding, the little sheep clamped on to them, bleating forlornly, and the sky with no light to it. The ancient heavy sense of it possessed her again, the timeless glimpse of it.

She stood there in the wonder of it, unmoving.

'Gone to sleep?' It was her husband behind her. She had not heard them return.

'Isn't she a funny one?' he said to her uncle, in a way of explanation. He was hot and excited with his sport by the brookside.

'You *must* go?' asked her uncle, dropping his eyes to her, strangely still and steady.

'I must,' she said.

'Yes,' he said. 'Perhaps so. Tell your dad. Plenty of time . . . ' He waved his hand upwards. He nodded in the old ancient way of his.

As they roared up the hill from the house, she saw him standing there, his dogs about him, his wide open face lifted.

# Janet Ifans' Donkey

He heard the heavy steps crunch up the gravel drive. It was the Sergeant coming with the summonses – he always came about this time. The Sergeant would leave him in peace at his dinner, and give him time for his cigar and then come in, very deferential, as clumsy as a horse, in his hobnail boots, carrying his helmet under his arm like a bowl.

He cocked his ear to listen, though he knew the step. Yes, the Sergeant had gone round to the side door as was his wont: there would be a bit of chaff with the housekeeper and then the solid, measured step down the corridor.

He pushed the things nearest him away, clearing the end of the table, and felt in his fob for his fountain pen. Then he shouted 'Come in' in a mixture of pleasantness and irritation.

The Sergeant took his seat beside the fire and spread his hands out over his knees. He was a big man, coarse cut, with a big, florid face and a moustache like a brush, which he kept swiping with his hand. He was very Welsh.

The little man raised his lack-lustre eyes in inquiry. He was never sure that the Sergeant was not laughing at him in some way. That was why he made such a show of authority. He was always glad when it was all over, when he had affixed

'Thomas Williamson', in his neat, business-like hand, at the bottom of these blue documents, and the Sergeant had gathered them up again like shares, and tied them up with the bit of string he kept twiddling about in his hand. There were other magistrates who could have done it just as well, he told himself, and yet the Sergeant came to him night after night. And that was not because he was chairman of the Bench, but because his house was nearest the police station; he knew that perfectly well: and he had a good idea that the Sergeant knew that he knew, in spite of his dumb show of deference.

'That all?' looking up, at the last summons.

'Yes, sirr.'

The Sergeant had his eyes on the decanter on the table, and, although he felt that it ought not to become a habit, he poured him out a glass. He always did.

'There is just wan thing, sirr . . . '

'Yes: yes?' he broke in irritably. He was not irritable; he was very pleased with himself, and with the day, but he wanted to show the Sergeant that he could not be trifled with and that his time was precious.

'About old Janet Ifans,' he went on. He brought a big hand backways across his moustache, gave a heavy sigh, and then bent the glass back over his nose.

'What!' said the little man, bristling.

'No – nothing, sirr. Nothing like that. Dead, sirr – yess, yess. All over now, sirr.'

'And . . . what has that to do with me?' he asked tartly.

He was not sure the Sergeant was not laughing at him. He looked uneasily into those thin, clear blue eyes in the florid face: they gave nothing away.

'No, sirr. Quite, sirr,' he broke in hurriedly. 'I understand, sirr.'

He had given himself away in spite of all. And he knew at once. He took another gulp at the port and swiped his moustaches as was his way when no words came.

The little man got up and walked to the big bay window, his back turned.

'Perhaps you had better explain,' he added drily.

'Not her, sirr. It's that bad old donkey – *ach y fi*. You don't mind me saying, sirr?'

'What *is* it?' He turned from the window. He was beside himself.

'Don't mind me saying, sirr?'

'Sergeant! *Please.* Will you please make yourself plain?'

'Yess, sirr.' He began at the beginning again. He looked down at his feet and stroked his moustache.

'The old woman go, sirr.' He waved his hand up briefly and then wagged his head. 'Time too! Time

45

for donkey too – but he very much alive. P.C. Jenkins go up there – go to shed. *Iesu mawr* – he kick. He try again. Eks-cuse me, sirr – he bite him in the backside. P.C. Jenkins come out.'

'Well?' said the little man, fuming.

'P.C. Jenkins – fery kind man. He throw in carrots.'

'What *do* you mean?' said the little man, very white.

'Well, sirr. What we do now? More carrots: then after, more carrots. From where? Policemen's allotments! How long? Ten, twenty years maybe. He a naughty donkey, sirr – he live for ever.'

'Sergeant,' he said, dropping his voice and wagging his head in his hurt. 'Really, Sergeant, I *must* ask . . . '

'Two things,' said the Sergeant, forced to the point. 'He live: he die. He live – where? He die – how?'

'I am afraid I have not the *slightest* idea of what you are talking about,' said the little magistrate, turning round to the light. He had set his face in his prim way, the smooth, round, little face like a white apple, with a hurt, petulant, little mouth and eyes wide and anxious, with blue rings round them like a macaw's. They called him Tommy Titt in the town, because of his sprightly little walk: when he had his hands in his trouser pockets and sent the tails of his frock coat out he looked like a tit, and when he was excited his voice went up high and shrill in a titter. He was an Englishman, and very wealthy, and they liked him more than most Englishmen, but he was sure they were always laughing at him. But then these Welsh people were altogether . . .

'Not the *slightest*,' he said again, shooting his hands out.

'All right, sirr,' said the Sergeant with a final nod, as he fumbled with the summonses. 'The old devil goes home tomorrow – to be sure.'

The little man raised his eyebrows in question. And the Sergeant rubbed his nose pensively and moved his feet about.

'A dirty job, sirr – *ach y fi*. How would you be getting a humane killer up against him, sirr? No, sirr. We got to pop a shot gun through the window.'

'No, no, no,' broke in the little man, raising his hands in horror.

'I was thinking, sirr . . . ?'

'Yes, yes?' he said in his exasperation.

'As perhaps a home might be found.'

'No doubt. We will see.' He nodded his head grimly. 'Is that all?' he asked.

'That's all, sirr.' The Sergeant made a great show of going.

'A pour old soul, sirr. No harm in her, like.'

'Yes, yes,' he said, hurrying him out in his anxiety.

'A bit of a character, if you understand, sirr.'

'Yes, yes,' he said again, waving his hands in his hurry.

'You remember, sirr . . . ?'

'Yes. Perfectly. Perfectly,' he said and went on saying 'perfectly, perfectly' as he strutted down the corridor. 'I will see what can be done. Come back later.' He only wanted to cut the Sergeant short, to get him out of the house.

The Sergeant was laughing at him: they were all laughing at him. He came back into the dining-room, his little white face strained and his eyes popping in his anger. No doubt the Sergeant had had his joke in the kitchen already. He was being laughed at in his own house. A vulgar, obscene old woman had dogged him ever since that time – ten years before – would always dog him.

He went over to the decanter for another glass of the old port. But he drank it at a gulp, not as he was wont to do in his happy, mellow after-dinner mind, a sip at a time and a heavy sigh. He was very proud of the port, proud of his judgment in it; he was proud of the house, of the lay-out of the gardens, of the shrubberies: he was proud of everything he saw – if he were only left to himself.

It was these outside things, like the visit of the Sergeant and this talk about the old woman, these things beyond him like the 'noises off' in a theatre, that upset him and left him bewildered. Life could be so very easy and pleasant – the old room, frayed and mellow, and the De Wint that he had picked up at a Shrewsbury auction: the glow of the fire and the book he had and the cigar waiting him, and a few details of the day's business which drifted across his mind quietly and placidly like the cigar smoke. Everything was so easy and comfortable as he liked it to be – as it ought to be – if one could only shut the door, shut out the outside. But then one had to do one's duty: that ominous word, duty, frightened him. He would not be without his sense of duty but the thought of it frightened him. Why all these foolish things happened he did not know – but they did happen, and they kept on happening.

He walked over to pull the bell cord in his agitation, but his hand stopped in the act. He did not want that woman laughing at him: they had probably had a good giggle below stairs. And here was he, a Justice of the Peace, and the wealthiest man in the town – yet a donkey could do this for him! It was absurd, he told himself – absurd. He walked about the room, his hands on his belly, saying absurd, absurd, many times over.

And then, as his mind went jumping about, he thought of her as he was bound to do. Things were better as they were, he told himself. They would never have got on together: it was just as well that they never tried.

But he had the image of her now – the clear, flame-like beauty of her, and the laughing, impudent eyes. She had gone through his life like a shooting star – a divinity that had brushed him with its wings. It was all so bewildering – it was all over before it started. It had never really happened. And, as he knew now, it could *not* have happened. She was not for him. But supposing . . . supposing – he kept turning it over in his own mind.

Supposing there had been no donkey, no vulgar old woman in the police court that day? She would have been here, a part of him, have come into his life, have broken it and irradiated it, like the colours on a spectrum. That bright, bewildering life – the life that might have been – frightened him and then excited him. But he wanted to feel that it could not have been, and he was sure that it could not have been.

There would have been no beginning and no end to that life: and he liked a beginning and he liked an end. All his life he had liked to know just where things were: and with her there was no knowing where things were – the sight of her, the sound of her laughter, was enough to send everything into a tumble.

'No, no,' he said out loud, wagging his head backwards and forwards. It would not do: it could not do. He went over to the sideboard for his cigar and bit the end off viciously, and then spat it into the fire. He looked for his book on some Assyrian excavations and then threw it down again: he did not feel like reading.

He had turned fifty now, and he was a bachelor. But he had always been a bachelor – then, when he might have married. He had been born a bachelor, and would die a bachelor, and he did not really care so very much. At that time he was forty – it was ten years ago – and he was as much a bachelor then as he was now. He could not think of any incursion into that prim, precise world that he had made his own.

How it had all happened he could never rightly remember: it was that 'county' dance that was the beginning of it. He was not 'county' but it was the first year of his mayoralty and he was very wealthy, and he was let in on sufferance. Elsewhere they would have called it the hunt ball, but in Wales, where everyone rode who could ride and had anything to ride, it would have been no better than letting in a troupe of beggars. So the county people had to get up an affair of their own which they called by some other name. It was held in the next town – it was always held in the next town, for there was a little pocket of county people round about, and it lay half-way over into Shropshire.

It was always the same – the old town hall, garlanded with flags and flowers, the band from Shrewsbury and the two hundred people, on and about the stairs, sipping claret cup and eating ices: the hot, laughing crowd and the parquet floor and the noise and the chatter.

That was when he met her – very suddenly on the stairs, with her laughing, wide open violet eyes and the straight, contemptuous stare at him as he stood there, transfixed. That was how it all began. She was the youngest daughter of a Welsh squire – they were as poor as church mice – and somehow or another things went on from that time. It was a 'match' before he had ever hoped that it might be: but the slightly amused, contemptuous stare never left her.

That was the beginning of it. He had then been in the county some ten or twelve years, the son of a business man in the Midlands, who had bought out one of the flannel mills on the Severn and put his son in as manager. That was in the days when there was a run on Welsh flannel, and within ten years the business had doubled its capital. It was now one of the biggest mills in the district and was his own.

He was already a rich man. He had begun by being rich and there was nothing more for him to do than become richer. He was an only son, and it seemed that everything came to him; but sometimes he felt that everything came to him; but sometimes he felt that everything passed him by. And yet all his life had been an orderly progress, but for this one thing that had tumbled him about so. He had never got over it, though he had told himself many times since that he had not been in love – that things would have been bound to go wrong. And now, as always, it left that ache, that sense of emptiness, of a life seen and never entered, like a small boy looking over a wall.

He was feeling it badly just now, all because of the Sergeant's visit, and mention of that confounded donkey and the old woman and all the rest of it. It puzzled and bewildered him – this sense of a life without, like the wind around the house, so wild and wayward, so wilful with no sense nor direction to it. He often felt like that on the Bench – that sort of peep-show view of a life that had no sense nor order. It was real enough, but it was very disturbing. He could never understand why people did the things they did.

He shuffled his feet into his carpet slippers and sank back into his easy chair, trying to remember all about it – as much as he dare – about old Janet Ifans and her donkey, and about the woman who might have been his wife.

Janet Ifans was an old woman who lived alone, a mile or two away from the town, in a little stone and slate cottage, perched like a toy over a dingle. Whenever she turned out the ash pan it fell down two or three hundred feet to the torrent below, and everyone said that some day Janet would go with it. But she never did, and she died in her bed.

She was a very old woman with a light blue eye, a very wicked eye, and a shrill, high voice, which you could hear fields away, like a jay screeching. She was always shouting at the poor old donkey who was her only companion. His name was Ebenezer, but he was always called Ebbe. She was the widow of an old soldier in the South Wales Borderers who had died from wounds received in some foreign war, and the Dandy Fifth had a guard of honour when he went, and fired a round over his grave.

They were very happy together, except that on Saturday nights he used to unscrew his cork leg and beat her with it, but she did not seem to mind very much, and they were always in chapel again on Sundays billing and cooing like a pair of turtle doves. They had both come from somewhere down South, in the heyday of the little town, and Janet was a very vulgar woman indeed when she liked, though, as the Sergeant had said, there was no harm in her, and she kept herself and the little house as bright as could be.

Every Saturday she went into the market with two baskets across the donkey, like panniers, filled with stuff from her little garden, and herbs that she sold in the town – mandrakes and dandelion roots, and such like. The journey in was easy enough, for it was down hill, but it was a different story coming back. And every Saturday night Janet was drunk, her wisp of grey hair blown across her face and her eyes wild, whacking the poor donkey across his rump and shouting abuse at him. He would trot for a few paces and then wait for her, and at the steep pitch she had to get her shoulder to him and give him a hoist up. And every Saturday he would always stop at the same place, with the old woman beating him with her umbrella, a crowd of little boys from the town behind her, shouting and laughing and throwing stones.

In the end people began to complain, because her language was very bad, but no one would do anything, for the old woman was ribald in her cups and she had a very quick wit. But when the Methodist minister intervened the story went round the town. She was a very strong Methodist, and she respected the cloth as nothing else in this world, but she was Janet Ifans, and that was all there was to it.

'Hush, hush, Janet *fach*. For shame on you,' he said, discovering her at the worst bit of the journey, using a lot of words in Welsh and English that he did not want to hear. He turned round and drove the naughty boys off with his stick and then came back to try and coax the donkey. But the donkey would not move, however much he tried, and he had to get his shoulder to it alongside Janet. And then it was that the donkey, not caring for this added persuasion behind him, gave a sudden start and they both fell down in the road – Janet with her legs in the air and her red petticoats down over her head and the minister hard on his haunches.

'*Uffern dân!* You old sow!' called out Janet after the donkey. She caught him by the tail and was for bringing him back to say he was sorry to Mr Edwards.

'Come back,' she shouted. 'Come back, you naughty old sow. Come back and say you're sorry to Mr Edwards *bach*. Haf a look and see the mess he iss in,' she shouted, helping the reverend gentleman to his feet. 'Take no notice, Mr Edwards *bach*. A shame on me, the naughty boy!'

The minister, who was a great heavy man with big feet like a policeman's, was the son of a farmer. He knew that drink and bad language were wicked, but he did not mind them very much if no one was about. And he had a big, round, raddled face that made one want to laugh. But the tip that he gave Janet was to prove his undoing. He told her that the next time Ebbe jibbed at the pitch she was to press the half of a lemon under his tail. This was said in the kindness of his heart, and to save Ebenezer unnecessary beatings. But a week or two later the old woman, having had her little drop, found him in the High Street after the weeknight service, with his deacons round him like a ring of nodding crows.

'Mister Edwards; Mister Edwards *bach* . . . '

She came rolling down the street, her umbrella raised.

'*Peidiwch*, Janet,' said the minister, raising his hand gently and calling on her to desist. He had no idea what was to come next.

'Oh fine, Mr Edwards!' she went on in her glory. 'I put the lemon – as you say.' She dropped her voice confidentially, her gin-laden breath going into their faces. She gave the old minister a playful nudge to show they understood one another. 'Up he goes!' She shot out her hands in sudden emphasis. 'Mis-terr Edwards – like a streak! *Iesu mawr* and I not keeping half a lemon to use myself. Mister Edwards and I neffer could catch him.'

That went to show what a rude old woman she was: her goings on were a byword. But no one ever thought of summoning her because she was just Janet Ifans, and everyone knew what Janet Ifans was. And she would never have been summoned at all, but for the donkey, and then it was not the donkey's fault. It was a silly joke that they played on her, and no one knew how far the joke was going to go.

After the market, when she had sold her little bits of vegetables and eggs, it was her custom to go round doing her shopping, and she always took Ebenezer with her, loading him up as she went. And on this particular Saturday she had cause to go into the china market, which was a place apart with straw on the concrete floor and all the china laid about, from the best Staffordshire sets to the ordinary things in everyday use – a cheap-jack among them like a hen among the eggs.

The old donkey was eating out of his nose-bag, quite happy in the rest, when some of the urchins of the town began playing tricks while the old woman's back was turned. They had sticks with pins on the end and they began prodding the donkey, one or two at a time, and then began to pull hairs out of his tail. At first he only scraped a hoof and lifted his head inquiringly, but as the torment increased he grew restive. And then they dropped a lighted jack-jumper under him and as the squib exploded he leapt in the air, bent in a buck, and with panic in his eyes made his way across the china.

But there was no way out and he went on in a wild stampede, crunching over dinner plates and sending mugs and china pots flying with his hoofs. Within five minutes he had wrecked the whole place: the floor was strewn with china splinters like confetti after a wedding; women were shrieking and the cheap-jacks shouting. When the Sergeant and another policeman arrived there was only the old lady left, chasing him round and round with her umbrella and trying to snatch at the bridle, all the while using the most foul language.

That was how she came to be summoned. It was the cheap-jacks who kept the Sergeant up to it, and he had no choice. She was charged with creating, or causing to be created, a breach of the peace and word of it went round. The whole town was behind Janet, who was a Welshwoman, and had never done anyone any harm, and why should the Salford Jews go and make trouble? No one asked them to come.

It was a gala day in the town on the Monday. There was going to be a bit of fun – besides, feeling ran very high. The sessions opened at eleven o'clock, but an hour before that the silver band had gone up the lane to meet her. The old lady came down in her tight black bodice with the stays showing, like a head out of an egg cup, and Ebenezer, hung about with garlands, braying at the trombones and showing his teeth.

It was the first day of the new chairman on the Bench. It was the one honour that was to come to him after the mayoralty – and it had come. It was the day of his life, and at his express wish his fiancée had come down to share his triumph. She had a seat beside the solicitors' table and she sat there with a faintly amused stare and the curl of a smile on her white oval face, at all the bustle and ceremonial.

It was the little man's day of triumph – the way he strutted out after the other magistrates and took

59

the centre seat, after a little bow to right and left and a wan smile at his fiancée. The oak seat was far too big for him; the varnished back of it stuck up behind him and he was lost in it. And before him the bar, separating the bench from the well of the court, was far too high, cutting him off at the collar so that he looked like a white-faced little boy peering over a fence. But he was as pleased as could be as the chief constable on behalf of the police, and then representatives of the law and the press, made their speeches of welcome.

Then began that ominous fanfare up the street, as the silver band approached and with it the procession and the confused murmur of voices. They had formed a ring outside the court and the band was ending up with 'The Cossacks', drowning every other sound within and without. The Sergeant went rushing out of the court, but he could do nothing: the music had to have its way. They had got the old woman tipsy and she was doing a jig in the street with her red petticoats lifted.

Within the court there was an inquisitive stare, as from one to another – all but the little man. Borne along on the crest of his triumph, he had some idea that the band was for him. He smiled down graciously at the astonished faces below him and was surprised at the lack of response.

A moment or two later, when the doors were

thrown open, the crowd swilled into the Town Hall and within a minute the court room was filled to the doors.

The clerk read through the first charge on the sheet; the Sergeant roared out 'Janet Ifans' and then, walking to the door, shouted down the stone corridor 'Janet Ifans'.

And then the fun began. It started the minute she entered the room, with her old shawl about her, the white hair blown across her face in a wisp and her eyes shining. As they walked down the gangway in the centre of the court, she caught hold of the Sergeant's arm and he could not shake her free. Then she shook her shawl over her head like a veil and went pattering along and simpering to the pews of people until there was uproar. As she went up into the dock she hitched up her petticoat, like a lady getting into a carriage, and then, once inside, waved her hand coyly to the Bench. There was uproar again.

The little man leaned over to the clerk, his face white and strained.

'Is she fit to plead?' he asked nervously. But things had now gone too far, and there was no going back. And the laughter never stopped: there was something fresh all the time. It was one long guffaw. The old woman had no idea what all the fuss was about and she kept questioning the Sergeant in Welsh, whilst he pointed to the Bench, trying to keep his face straight.

'How plead you – guilty or not guilty?' sang out the clerk.

The old woman leaned forward and repeated the question.

'There's daft!' she said and made to get out of the dock in her annoyance, but the Sergeant held on to the door.

'What's he want, then?' she shouted.

'What are you?' bellowed the Sergeant. 'You hearr what he says.'

'What am I?' she shrieked and then turned to the Bench with her umbrella raised. 'I give you what for. No one says one word to me since Seth go. No back doors for me, Mr Benbow: no indeed. I know!' She wagged her finger viciously at the little cross-eyed clerk below her.

'Guilty or not guilty: yes or no?' roared the Sergeant, helping her out.

'What the matter with *you* – you old bullock?' she said, turning on him.

'She pleads guilty, your worships,' explained the Sergeant after a lot of bother.

'Worships!' she broke in. 'What worships? I know every wan of them.'

She began making an inventory from left to right, touching up their private lives with many rude and bawdy details until they managed to stop her.

But it was hopeless, and they could do nothing

with her. They had got her in the dock and they could not get her out – not without going on with it all. And all the time the court was in an uproar.

The little man sat there, his fingers laced and his round head sunk forward on his chest. It could be no worse, he felt. He had never known such humiliation as this in all his life. He dared not look up. But he felt that *she* was laughing too. He knew that she was laughing without looking at her. And this knowledge – that she would be bound to laugh, was not beside him in his humiliation – hurt him more than the humiliation itself. There was a great distance between them – how great he did not know. But he felt it now – the hopelessness of it.

That ribald crowd below him – that was one thing. To them law and justice and the decencies of life – it was something to get fun out of, some sort of a game. But he felt that she ought to know better. And yet he knew it was not a question of knowing better: it was a different way of looking at things. It was a different world that he could not enter – and he had no wish to enter. He felt alone, absolutely alone, among these people: they had their own way of doing things and they ought to be left to themselves.

It was in all this uproar that he heard her speak. She had stood up at the table, in that impulsive way of hers, but her large, lustrous eyes, with that impudent gleam in them, had suddenly clouded.

She was sorry – but she was not sorry for him.

'May I try?' she asked.

She looked along the Bench from one to another and then her eyes came to rest on him, waiting for the nod. But the others had nodded all along the row before him, and his nod was only a matter of form. He knew, as he nodded, that it had nothing to do with him.

Then she stood up and faced the old woman, her face set and resolute. As thought at a command, the tumult stopped. The Vaughans were a very old family and one of themselves. And the old lady became as docile as a lamb. If Miss Vaughan had something to say it was different.

The young woman spoke in Welsh, pleading with her and sounding her lovely lilting voice through all shades of expression, anger, reproach and then a half hidden command.

The little man raised his eyes in wonder: he had never heard her like this – that something in the voice that transformed it. He could not understand a word that she said, and yet, in a way, he was able to follow her. There was a loving, intimate touch to it all that confounded him: the aristocrat and the peasant, the vulgar old woman in the dock, engaged in this pleasant preliminary banter.

What she said was something like this:

'Janet, dear. You must not be naughty. No indeed! The gentlemen don't want to harm you.

They only want to know how it was that Ebenezer kicked the plates. That is all. Don't be afraid, Janet, for we are all with you. Just say what happened and how the naughty boys gave him a fright. *Ach*, naughty boys they were. Tell the little man in the middle all about it – just in your own words – and everything will be all right. Now be a good girl, Janet, and do as I tell.'

The old woman nodded approvingly, called her a little dear, and began to say how she knew all the family and what a fine family they were, and then the young woman put her finger to her lips and pointed to the chairman.

'In your own words,' she said in English.

The old woman turned herself round to the Bench and coughed into her hand once or twice. Then she turned to the young woman again:

'Where to start?' she asked.

'At the beginning,' nodded the chairman, trying to smile. 'Just how it happened.'

'Happen!' she shouted. 'Indeed, sirr, there wass no happen. It end before it happen – so there!'

She was beginning to get truculent again but the young woman once more put her finger to her lips and Janet just as suddenly subsided. In the blank row of faces on the Bench she saw only the little man offering comfort, so she addressed herself to him.

'No, sirr. I tell you. Ebbe – a good boy, Ebbe.

Fery good boy. No one say anything bad about Ebbe. *No indeed*, sirr.'

She began to wag her head backwards and forwards at the memory.

'Poor lit-tel boy,' she said, her voice warming to it. Then she looked straight at the magistrate, her thin blue eyes alight.

'Now I ask, sirr, I ask you straight. Suppose, sirr, as how naughty boys go put a cracker under your bottom, sirr – right and left!'

'Silence!' roared the Sergeant, running down the court. He kept sweeping his hands downwards, trying to get the people to their seats. No one heard what he said: no one cared. Roar on roar filled the room. The Bench sat there, glum and silent, smirking into their hands. The little man, his head bowed, his face bloodless, waited to be heard.

'Case dismissed,' he got out at last.

Even so, no one heard him. The Sergeant ran forward and leaned his head over.

'Case dismissed!' he roared, opening the dock gate and shooing the old woman out. Then he went on to clear the court, driving them before him like a flock of sheep.

The old woman stepped primly out of the dock and then preened herself in the court. She was a bit bewildered by it all – only knowing that in some miraculous way it was all over, and that she could go home. And she was sure that Miss Vaughan was at the bottom of it – the nice lady that she was.

'*Diolch yn fawr, Miss Vaughan bach,*' she said with great fervour, wringing her by the hand.

But the young lady was very serious now.

'You be a good woman, Janet, and go straight home,' she said with a wan little smile.

He waited until the other magistrates had left the court before he came out of the retiring room. The big Town Hall was empty now, save for the Sergeant, busying himself with pens and pencils at the table at the far end. She was there, waiting for him.

'I am . . . sorry,' he said. It came out in a little gulp. He could say no more. He kept his eyes on the floor.

'No,' she broke in, during the long silence. 'I am sorry.'

'Thank you,' he said, and then again, 'Thank you.'

He knew that she was sorry for him – sorry in her heart. And he knew, too, that she had always been sorry for him.

'I suppose . . . ' he began as they walked towards the door. He searched his heart in his misery, but no words came.

'Oh,' she said, '*that* can wait. Some other time,' she added, trying to lighten the load.

But he knew then that it was all over.

He awoke with a start when the Sergeant returned, and looked round the room in bewilderment. The book lay spread out on the floor beside him, and the fire had burned low. He must have had a nap – a most unusual thing for him. But he could not quite remember whether he had slept or not – whether he had dreamt or not. He knew that he had been thinking of her in some sort of a way. And it seemed to him now that she belonged to a dream – that she had never entered his life, and never could have entered it. It seemed to him stranger than ever that such things could happen, that such and such a thing was really within his grasp, when it was always beyond it. And yet . . .

'You told me, sirr . . . to come back.'

The Sergeant was standing there, large and florid, half in and half out of the door. The maid had taken him up.

'Yes, yes,' he said petulantly. 'What is it now?'

'The donkey, sirr – as belonged to old Janet Ifans.'

The little man rubbed his eyes awake.

'Yes, yes. Of course.'

He straightened himself in his chair and beckoned the Sergeant in.

'Well . . . ?' he went on acidly. 'What about this . . . this confounded donkey?'

'I told you, sirr,' said the Sergeant reproachfully.

'Well then. I forget.'

'Well, sirr. The old boy must go. Pity, sirr – but there it is.'

'Then why ask *me*?' answered the little man, nettled.

'Well, sirr; it's not nice: no indeed. To blow a hole in the old thing. And for why?'

'Oh no, no,' broke in the little man at the horror of it. 'Not *that* – surely not that.'

'Well, sirr. That's how it is,' went on the Sergeant placidly.

'But surely . . . surely you can find someone to take it?'

'Who?' The Sergeant fixed him with his raw eye.

'Well!' he said, shocked. 'There's not a great deal of Christian charity about – seemingly.'

'No, sirr – not for donkeys.'

'All right,' he said with a final heave. He waved the Sergeant to the door. And he was sure that the Sergeant had known all along what would happen.

# The Shearing

All down the two sides of the barn they went, sitting straddle-legged on rough untrimmed benches, their backs against the loose stone walls. Sometimes they would move a sheep across their knees and start the talk going, without raising their heads.

The place stank with the warm sweat reek of fleeces: they lay there in a growing heap as one man after another, with a final flick of the shears, tossed them on to the stone floor.

They had come in on ponies across the mountains and from the valley farms to lend a hand with the shearing, as they in turn would be so helped themselves.

For the short, harsh spring of the Welsh coast was mellowing into the milder summer and the sheep were going up to the mountain shorn of their wool. And the natural gaiety of the people kept pace with the seasons. In this farm near the village the men were telling the old stories or fashioning new ones with native wit: without in the yard was the commotion of boys miching from school while from in the old farmhouse itself came the raised laughter of women, making their own fun in the big kitchen, as they busied themselves with the men's food.

Two boys were running endlessly carrying in

the sheep. They carried them as they would a child, their bellies up, and laid them down on benches for ever emptying. Only in between times would a man find time for talk, wiping the reek off his hands and leaning his back to the wall as he looked about him.

The old farmer had let go his sheep. It went scuttling through the open door with the lads holding on to the shorn neck as they raced her without, on to the commotion of voices around boiling cauldron of pitch. The old man wiped his brow with the gesture of a job well done and looked across to his young neighbour. And then, in the casual way of small talk:

'So married life is all right then, Lewis John?'

'Not bad.'

And the lad, whose wild young face set as though there frozen, buried his head still deeper in the fleece before him.

And it was not all casual as it seemed. The old man brought his hand with a comic gesture backwards across his nose and winked around him. He was a great wag and what people call a character, an old man now of seventy but still good for his fifty sheep a day, and all done clean, which was a good deal more than any of the others. There was no harm in John Shadrach Ifans, or John Shad as he was to everyone, with his round, fresh, crab-apple face and the sharp blue eyes that missed nothing, always a-twinkle; the white, untidy hair ruffled up heedless on his head; the long, white, arrogant curve of his moustache that gave the face some semblance of age.

At the same time they thought he was skirting near thin ice, and secretly enjoyed the prospect of what was to come. Not one of the others dared have gone so far, but then he had the privilege of age and again of innocence.

'Not bad!' went on the old man, as though taking the words from him and turning them over. 'Well, well, that is one way of putting it, I suppose.' He looked around him again with the same show of dumb innocence. 'When I was a young man I thought it very good.'

And again he rubbed his nose with that sly, backward swipe and reached his tongue out slowly round his cheeks and went on:

'Life is very unfair – to the young people, I mean. Now if I had to choose between coming here and a warm feather bed at the farm of Tŷ Newydd I *think* perhaps the bed would win. In all this world there is no place like the bed.'

'*Myn ufferni* – you ought to know: you have been in plenty.'

For the first time the lad raised his head from out the sanctuary of the sheep's belly. There was the quick, bright flash of a smile that seemed to shed light around him. He nodded, knowing that he had scored, and as though to say he was going to play their own game for once and keep his temper on a leash. This was his first initiation into the old hierarchy of married men and he had to submit to the baiting of his elders with as good a grace as he could. And if that was all there was to it, then he was going to let it pass.

'In my time – in my time,' mused the old farmer, not taking it amiss. He clamped his gums together and spoke as to the wall, and his eyes went off into distance. 'And the happiest days of my life, too, *and* most men know it.'

He was talking to them all now, half banter half serious, with the warm intimacy that their own tongue gave. And for all its frankness it was natural to them as the light they saw or the food they ate, that ancient, undiscoverable life of the mountain farms, which Christianity had touched but not altered. Even in the rapt ecstasy of redemption that followed the first revivals, this old worn, pagan life endured: the things of the earth, the ways of a man with women, these they knew as the psalmist did, for it was their life.

'Well, well, Nature, after all.'

He was a man named Wili Owain and the thin and rather foolish white face was set gravely, as though to hold in the weight of thought, and a mouth without meaning was clamped down hard in a judicious line. He was no match for these two and the profundity was meant to ease out the distance.

'Nature – ah, Nature!'

The old man calmly pulled out the torn strips of rag from between his teeth and, crossing the ewe's legs, bound them up, and then settled her on his knees. He rubbed a hand softly over the fleece to search for a beginning, prodding carefully with his shears into the thick wool of the neck: a few careful snips and the fleece fell open, and, like a furrow ripped in dirty water, the shears went down the belly to the tail. The fleece fell apart, trailing its ragged edges almost to the floor: what was once a furrow widened, as the uncovered belly showed itself, the short virgin wool beneath as white as drift snow.

He raised his head a moment, and then, looking to the lad Lewis John beside him and as though the young wild head that tossed restless in its life gave him a tag on which to hold his sermon, went on, with a quiet munching of chops:

'She is a funny old girl is Nature – as stubborn as a woman, and just as contrary. And you can trust Her just about as much, boys *bach!* For she is thinking in her way and we, poor fools, go on thinking in ours. And who is right, think you?'

He tossed this over to them as some stray morsel which in the process of time should be considered, simply for its own sake. And to start them off, and in one of those abrupt changes from the joking to the serious-minded in the way of the Welsh, he leaned forward and raised a free hand over his head, wagging a finger solemnly into space. And then his voice, like a preacher filled with the spirit, went mounting up in invocation:

'And who is right, *m'achgen'i*? Nature, in all her wonderful glory who sendeth the spring into the valleys and giveth drink to every beast of the fields: yea, yea, who appointed the moon for seasons and who toucheth the hills and they smoke . . . or Lewis John Williams of the farm of Tŷ Newydd in the parish of Pantymaen?'

'Me again!'

'I am only *saying*, my boy, for the sake of illustration. It is the same with all of us.' He stroked his chin again in the same sly way. 'Unless perhaps Llew Pryce here who is too timid . . . '

'Give me a chance, that's all.'

The quiet youth, as though startled into speech, raised his head laughing, in a show of braveness.

'You have had plenty, so they tell me. Only when the girls begin to think things, off he runs to his mam, and that is no good to anybody.'

The sound of low laughter, of men pleased within themselves, rose around the high metallic snip of shears. They did not raise their heads, only grunted over their work. There was too much to do. And the old man might catch their eye and out would come a sally at their expense, which they did not want at all.

'Oh, no, that is no good to anybody,' went on old John Shad, heaving the sheep over on his knees. 'Lewis John is better than that, I must say. He knows the way to the ladies' hearts and once you have touched their hearts there is no knowing what . . . or so they tell me.'

He raised his worn head a moment and cocked a live eye at the young man before him.

'Hush, hush – fair play. He is a married man now,' one of the men broke in.

There was always a time when things began to get out of hand, when a sally with the point of truth in it got home. So the old man, free of the sheep at last, tossed up his hands in a casual way, and in a voice meant to condone all things said simply:

'Wild oats! And better when you are young – a spring sowing, *whatever* the harvest. Ay, Lewis John?'

The lad winced as under a blow and his head jerked up from his work, flung up in anger: the sheep he held reared up her dumb head in a frantic heave.

'Ah – you've touched her, Lewis *bach*.'

The old man pointed his shears-end to the soak of fresh blood that spread out on the white, shorn belly.

'Hell – can't I see?'

Lewis John threw the shears on the bench before him and, not waiting for the oil bottle but with one brief glare around him, shouted:

'Look here, Mr Ifans, – that's enough for one day! Now leave it alone!'

Then he flung himself out through the door.

'Tut, tut – so childish,' went on old John Shad as though nothing had happened. Then he looked round to the others with the same old, all-comprehending look. 'And everyone *knows*, boys *bach*, which is small wonder as she is a girl of this parish. And whatever his wife might like to think or say that girl was *not* brought to bed by the fairies!'

'She is here today,' a man said, in the same way of small talk.

'What! Gwenna?'

The old man's head went up as though startled out of himself: then he cocked it as though trying to distinguish between the shrill laughter of women in the kitchen. Then back to the same easy tone: 'Well – that is awkward, boys *bach*, to say the least . . . but they are bound to meet sometime, after all.'

He waved his hands up in the same off-handed way but it was still on his mind: he shook his head several times as though to wipe out the memory of it. These days of shearing, when all came in a spirit of good-fellowship, were soon over as it was. It was a pity to see one spoilt. But they were back again to the old talk.

'As though the folk at Tŷ Newydd will let a small thing like *that* worry them – now that they have got Blodwen off! *Myn ufferni*, you would think, to hear them talk, that Lewis John had wings, instead of a son by another woman,' broke in Wili Owain in a bitter challenge.

And with the empty seat before them the tongues were loosened and they began to argue among themselves, taking sides as they were bound to do in a thing which touched the village, and its honour, so deeply.

They could not help liking the lad Lewis John still – would have done much to excuse him if only they could. For he was one of those men who do not belong to themselves but to the people: his quick tongue and nimble wit, the flashing, open tilt of mischief in his face, forestalled the angry word. And after some fresh, some daring piece of devilment, there was only a wise nodding of heads and an indulgent holding-up of hands:

'Goodness only knows what we shall make of him.'

And yet no one really wanted him otherwise and so one and all continued to give false evidence to river watchers and angry policemen and he took it all quite cheerfully as his due, promising to behave next time – and with a great show of hurt innocence.

And now the old happy days had gone. He was

quick to sense it and it gave a fresh edge to him.

'No,' picked up old John Shad, 'the Tŷ Newydd folk are not going to let a small thing like that worry *them*.'

Beyond the words the old man sounded his voice so that it had a faintly unfamiliar air of deference that chilled. And it was noticed they were always referred to as the 'Tŷ Newydd folk', never in the more homely way that warmed.

'Well, he's done well for himself, whatever,' broke in the timid man Llew Pryce, which only provoked Wili Owain to a fresh shout:

'I tell you Gwenna is worth ten of her, any day of the week, *and* she has not two thousand pounds fastened on to her knickers.'

'Now, now. That is unfair – that is unfair,' old John Shad broke in with a gesture of peace. There was bound to be a row – always had been since it happened.

'And two hundred pounds spent on a wedding does not make it any the more *right* – no, nor photos in the *County Times*!' went on Wili Owain in the full flood tide of his indignation. He began beating with the end of his shears on the bench beside him, trying to make himself heard. The three Methodist ministers, the two hundred guests with printed invitation cards, the dinner for the poor in the County Workhouse – he waved his hands dismissing it all, and then leaned over and spat out through the open door. And on a high note of piety:

'Oh, no – a *poor* girl has nothing to offer but herself . . . '

'*Myn ufferni* – that's enough, too.'

The sudden burst of laughter that greeted old John Shad's sally eased the feeling between them, and some of the old intimacy came back.

'We are all very foolish indeed, boys *bach*.' It was old John again. 'The best thing is to marry a girl for love . . . who has got money though not because . . . '

Again he brought his hand backwards across his nose in the familiar mischief-making swipe. But Wili Owain was now in the full flood-tide of righteousness:

'He did not do the right thing, boys *bach*, and mark my words, no good will come of this other.'

He brought the shears-end a resounding blow on the bench again and glared round with a light of challenge in his eye. Then leaning towards the door:

'Tŷ Newydd folk indeed!'

And he spat outside with the passion of the righteous.

It was hard to know why the Tŷ Newydd folk were not liked. They had made money, which was a good thing, and they had made it out of the English – and that was better still. And what was more they had come back to spend it in the district where they had been born and bred. And yet their own people no longer knew them: they had taken fresh root elsewhere. They knew the old man simply as Tomos Richards, one-time cowman at Tŷ Newydd, and his wife Sara as the servant girl there. They were simply London Welsh milk-men with 'pots of money', even though they had bought the farm in which they once worked. It did not put them back on the land. And Sara knew this, though it did not daunt her. She was an ambitious woman and in some ways a dangerous one and she straightaway set herself the hard task of making herself somebody: her grim, big-boned face with the few sparse hairs of a moustache, her sour, unlighted eyes and the shorn hair which was to keep her for ever young at sixty, was seen everywhere, often enough trailing around her daughter Blodwen.

'Sara had a little lamb' began one of the local *penillion* and it ended up on a bawdy note, of how Sara had found the little lamb a man. For Blodwen, a spoilt child and oversexed to boot, was not so discriminating as her mother. So ran the local gossip and it was usually right.

Nevertheless Sara was a character, entitling her to her maiden name, and though they laughed at her it was only to hide their fear. And she was a person of some importance, on almost all committees, a magistrate and a deaconess in

Shiloh, the Calvinistic Methodist chapel from which she had been married in the long ago. And with her head bobbing in the chapel vestry or over the tea urn in the Sunday School or with two or three people about her in the street, they knew something was going on, though what that something was did not always reveal itself.

It did not seem likely that scandal would ever touch her or hers but she reckoned without Blodwen. Lewis John was going through an awkward time just then: hard things were being said about him. Perhaps it was to spite the parish (which he saw settling on him for ever and ever) or perhaps it was the inducement of the great outside world which he had glimpsed on a short spell of lorry-driving. Or it may have been Blodwen herself, who was attractive enough in a spitefully passionate way. But there is no doubt that she made a fool of herself and Lewis John, who was used to shaking the tree for the fruit to fall, did not mind it coming otherwise. People began to talk. In the end Sara took a hand. She had hoped for a doctor or at least a minister, but the lad, even to her own hostile eye, was presentable enough, like some lanky pup with the promise of turning out well.

There was only one thing in the way – this unhappy affair with Gwenna that still dragged itself on in the life of the village.

'Trust Sara,' they said, with a grim nodding, and

they were right. For in ways that no one quite knew, and without ever anything being said in so many words, people were now beginning to believe that perhaps Gwenna was not all that they had thought she was. It came as a shock to people who had known her since childhood but then, it was explained, she was "at an awkward age". And as for poor Lewis John, – well, 'you know what he is.' And as they most certainly did, they found themselves forgiving him much.

And now for the first time doubts were being thrown on the child's father and it was even said that Lewis John would have a solicitor to defend himself, though everyone knew where the money would come from. And as that young man could believe anything he wanted to believe he was very nearly a party to it. Let it be said to his credit that it did not go any farther. Though stubborn to the end, he suffered an order to be made on him in the court.

'The Tŷ Newydd folk!' said Wili Owain again, wiping his mouth. 'And as for Blodwen, she is a silly bitch – nothing more nor less.'

'Now, now.'

' . . . and she can have what is coming to her, for that sort of thing doesn't pay, boys *bach*.'

He looked around him with the same glare of righteousness and smacked a fist into the palm of his hand.

*'Uffern!* Here she comes,' someone whispered, and his mouth stayed open in the midst of speech. Into the uneasy quiet that descended on them old John Shad's voice was raised in nonchalant greeting:

'And how does Mrs Blodwen say she is on this fine summer morning? Come in – come in and let us see you.'

He waved her towards them with his shears. The woman in the doorway was getting on for thirty, though the long, sullen face and big eyes, the passionate pout of the thick, childish mouth, made her look younger. She had long, thin, neurotic hands that were never at rest, pulling and unpulling at her gloves, and all the time she was moving from one foot to the other. She was dressed well but without real taste and her pale face was touched with scarlet in a way that one does not expect in the country, giving a ghoulish look to her brittle type of prettiness.

'Oh, I only . . . is Lewis John about?'

The old man waved his hands to the outside.

'He was,' he ventured.

'Was!'

And then the wide, staring eyes were flecked with panic. She jerked her head around her, unbelieving, and then tugged at her gloves again.

'Where . . . where has he gone, then?' she got out, trying to keep the voice steady.

'Well, Blodwen *fach*, where *would* he go, think you?' He held her with his drooping, shadowed eyes as though peering into her very heart. And then, after the cruel pause, with no more than a hint of the coming smile: 'To no harm, surely? A breath of fresh air to cool that hot young head of his would be fairly near the mark.'

The held breath let itself out in the relief.

'Oh, I . . . I see.'

Yet she was not sure. She looked around them again, looked in the dumb, polite faces for some answer that would never come.

'Any message?' went on the old man, in the same casual way.

'No – I'll call again.'

And then she had picked her way across the muddy yard, holding her tailored coat down over her knees in answer to the rude wind always blowing. A moment later they heard the little car rattle off along the lane.

'*Myn ufferni* – she is afraid of letting him out of her sight – *and* you know why!'

Wili Owain, come back to speech, nodded in his disgust.

And then old John Shad took up again:

'Well, she is wiser than you think; she knows what Lewis John has done once he can do again. And though Gwenna has had her lesson you know how they say: it is easy to light a fire in an old hearth. And somehow I don't think those two would be long in striking up the tinder, boys *bach*: though she is too good for him, – made of tougher stuff.'

And he let his mind wander off to the little thing she had been, wild and headstrong with her bit lip and her triumphant, tossing head, the black hair flung loose in defiance.

'Dai Jim, where did you get this little heifer with you?' was his standing joke with her old grandfather, and the old man always had some answer ready. He would give her away for nothing, or for half a crown, depending on how she had behaved herself that day.

As his mind wandered off to her and then to the old grandfather and then to the whole brood of the Vaughans he lifted his weathered face, with the no longer merry eyes, and a sad, hurt smile went over it.

'Silly to themselves,' he said almost aloud and he shook his white, unruly head grimly and his lean mouth puckered up as though under a blow. for his mind had gone off from them to life and all its hard bargaining and he was sorry for them, sorry as for no one else in this world. They were not the people for that: it was as though they were laughing at life, sometimes grimly enough but always laughing, and that nothing would ever bring them face to face with its awful seriousness.

Well, they had paid for it and perhaps it was only right that they should. And yet it hurt him that it had to be so: all that big family in a four-roomed cottage and old Dai Jim, with a few years left him, still at work in the quarry: come back, he had, from the pits in South Wales when his only son was killed, so that he could give the children a fresh start.

And then at the same time he felt an old joy warm him and his hand quivered over the fleece as though stricken, joy to think that in some way they were never down, that nothing in this life could ever make them less than what they were.

'Poor old Dai Jim, it is a hard thing to stomach all the same,' he ventured as he let his thoughts wander on. He could feel for the old man; of all the children left on his hands Gwenna was the one: the old man's spirit and the old man's wit had gone on to her – yes, and the old man's innocence, as though to level things up.

Old Dai Jim was going to give the lad a thrashing – paternity orders he did not understand. He understood asking a man outright what he was going to do, and knocking some sense into him if there was any nonsense. He had a sack over his bent shoulders and he was off down the village when he was first told. The neighbours, however, had warned the minister and he was there to stop him.

'Dai Jim, your old fighting days are over: you have been called to the Lord.'

And the old man surveyed his great gnarled hands that in his days down south had battered their way through three valleys, emblem of the sorrow and pride of the old-time triumphs when he was any man's man for a quart.

*'Myn ufferni* – pity I left my tools behind!'

And there was the same quick flash of a smile that took off his temper, and a moment later he was talked back into reasonableness, as they knew he would be.

He went on hoping that some sign of manliness in Lewis John would show itself. And he kept on hoping when Gwenna was brought to bed. There was not much Lewis John could do then but show his face: but that was what was expected of him, for it was a near thing. When the district nurse after twelve hours of it sent for the doctor the old women on the doorsteps began to nod their heads gravely.

'It's up to her now,' they said, wondering whether her strength would hold. And old Dai Jim never moved from the range, staring into the red, sullen glow and wiping off the sweat that stood out like dew on his great battered head, his mouth trying to fashion some rough prayer that should not be sounded. When the feeling got too much for him he would let go a breath like a steam escaping and then raise his head quickly as though nothing had happened. It was not his way to show what he felt.

It was the longest day he had ever known. The roads were all snowbound, the topmost bits of hawthorn on the hedges showed up out of the drifts like black rush clumps: over all the mountainside the piled stone walls ran like faint pencil markings in the billowing white. Yet the doctor, who was one of the old school, did get through.

'She is bred the right way, Dai Jim,' was all he said as he came downstairs.

The old man got up and grasped his hand and then flung his head aside.

'There is a cup of tea waiting,' he said with a wave to the table.

Old Dai Jim liked the lad: he made all allowances. One had to come to it of one's own accord and though it was a bad beginning, two young people who were fond of one another would get over that. And they *were* fond of one another. The whole village knew it. It was not somebody he had picked up on a Fair Day night.

And then he heard of this other wedding to be and he seemed to break up overnight. He could not understand it and they had to tell him over and over again; he could not believe that such things were.

And so to that last wretched stage of all – the court. They could do what they liked now, for once it got there it was the end of everything.

But it would place the child's father beyond all doubt, they argued, and now that the Richardses were behind Lewis John it was just as well. It was their doing that the whole thing had got to the court at all.

And it was soon over. The chairman of the Bench made one last plea for them to come together, turning his wide, sorrowful eyes from one to another: the silent lad, stiff with a hurt pride, and the woman to whom he dared not raise his eyes, filling the magistrate's sad heart with the wonder of all unspoilt things.

'It is a great pity to see young people . . . like this.'

He raised his head once more and turned his eyes to the lad as though to implore him.

'Is there no way at all?'

Lewis John looked up from his feet and shook his head.

'No sir – none at all.'

Gwenna gripped on to the witness-box, stiffening as she stood. It was as though a lash had struck her in the face. Was it for this, then, that she had been persuaded to come, so that Lewis John could tell the world that he had finished with her? For a moment the dark, brimming eyes went wider as though unbelieving and then she knew that it was true. It was beyond her understanding but it was true. Things had happened in these few short months that seemed no part of life at all, as though everyone had, in some way, gone out of their minds. So they could talk if they wanted. And a moment later she had flung up her head, with the old spirit shining in the straight, set eyes. They were harder now than they had been, but she was learning a great deal that she had never thought to learn.

That was all, except that her solicitor rose and explained:

'I'm afraid there is an explanation, sir. This young man's affections, for reasons best known to himself, have been transferred elsewhere.'

And the people in the court turned as one, with neck-craning stares, to where Blodwen and her mother sat, staring stolidly into the glum silence.

That was the last time that they were face to face. And who would ever say that they would meet again? Even Blodwen told herself now that it could not, would not, happen. And yet she was not sure. There was the child and there was Gwenna – a shawl around in the old Welsh way of nursing – whenever she went into the village. She had always been a lovely girl but, with that quiet, incommunicable pride of the young mother as though a bud were slowly widening out into life, she was lovelier than ever. It seemed as though this girl was the wife and it seemed sometimes as though the girl knew it. And Blodwen's jealous nature would not let it rest. It began in a small way and seemed to gather to itself fresh torments. She was making herself ill and sometimes she feared for her reason. What was not there she invented: she *knew* now that it was bound to happen for she had told herself so until at last she was sure of it, as of nothing else in this world. And like in some lurid, edgeless dream she tortured herself to be able to see what she dreaded seeing.

'You are not looking too well these days, Blodwen *fach*.'

The old woman in the village shop, like a great black bird slowly sunning itself, heaved out a sigh and her black stuff blouse rose and fell with it. Dear me – there was plenty of trouble in the world, she seemed to say, without having to listen to the old, old story all over again. And then, more gruffly than she meant:

'Why *are* you so silly?'

But the next moment she was hobbling round the counter for the young wife had fallen into a chair and was near hysterics.

'Oh God – why was I born?' she kept repeating, dabbing her eyes as though to hide out the light of day. She said it in so hopeless a way, so dry and empty a voice, that the old woman, who knew all the wretched story, found her heart touched in spite of herself.

And in the back room, with a cup of tea to revive her, she turned up her hollow eyes in a helpless plea.

'He's not there. I was in the barn just now and he's not *there!*'

She went on wringing the tiny knot of handkerchief until the blood left the helpless hands. She had said too much: she bowed her head in shame. A tiny stretch of colour came into the white face. She had never been as bad as this before: she was getting worse and worse.

'And you know what Lewis John is? With a bit of skirt about.'

The old woman raised her head and pushed the steel spectacles up from the old ringed-around eyes that had now gone hard with a warning glare. She held her white-boned hands up so that there should be no mistake. 'Now that is quite enough of that.'

The wife, sensing the change, got up stiffly from the little wicker chair, preening herself in a new pride.

'She just *happened* to be there, like,' she got in.

'Good gracious, woman!' The old shopkeeper's softly chewing chaps set in anger. And then she stopped herself. 'Indeed, truth, if you go on like this you will throw them into one another's arms and it will be your doing, my girl.'

It was no good talking, as she knew. Instead she drew in a deep breath and sighed once more, as she heard the shop door slam. Where on earth she was off to now no one knew except that she was not going home. To the barn again no doubt.

'*Dir anwyl* – there will be some doings before the day is out,' she said out loud.

The old woman waved her hands in the same forlorn way: she was too old now, she seemed to say, for this sort of thing.

But in the barn the men were busy. Like grasshoppers in chorus the steel clippers went on, the rumble of voices or a sharp angry rebuke, the sudden commotion of a bolting sheep loosed too soon. The fleeces, folded and packed tight into parcels of wool, stood in an ever-towering heap in the middle, and out in the by-take and beyond that again, in the lower skirt of the mountain, the new-white sheep were straggling up in a thin line.

After a time Lewis John had come back and taken his old place on the bench. He sat there drumming on his knees waiting for them to bring him a sheep. For some time no one spoke – it was difficult to make a place for him after the outburst. Once the intimate note had gone it was hard to sound again.

But at last old John Shad, with no show of interest:

'Your missis has been here, Lewis John.'

'And what the hell has that got to do with you, then?'

'Tut, tut, tut!' The old man made a noise with his mouth and wagged his hands deploringly. He had meant it as a gesture of friendship, he seemd to say, and look what return he had had.

'I only said she had been here – surely a man can open his mouth?'

'Not your sort of mouth, John Shad.'

The lad nodded towards him in a tight-lipped threat and the old man, finding it hard to stomach the insult:

'If she was to put a bit of rope around you . . . But leave him alone and he'll come home, wagging his tail behind him.'

The lad jumped up, sending the bench flying to the wall. He held his clenched fists trembling at his sides.

'*Iesu mawr*,' he got out through his clenched teeth and swung his arms about him in an empty rage. Then, reaching a taut finger at the old man:

'Only for your age, John Shad, I would . . . oh . . .'

He ended up on a note of glory and bent his arms up with the still trembling fists.

'Age, indeed! They are always either too young or too old for you, Lewis *bach*.'

This was a reference to Gwenna: those around looked up with a quick, anxious glance. One or two

95

of them ran between the men, but old John Shad sat there with the dignity age gave.

'I have thrashed better men than Lewis John – when they were men.'

He made a heave towards the old man, struggling to free himself from the men who held him.

At that moment the barn filled with shadow and they all instinctively looked to the door. His wife was there. The men let go their hold, let their hands fall down sheepishly beside them. Old John Shad heaved himself round in his seat and craned his neck to see the cause of the sudden transformation. And then, with an old courtesy that was part of him:

'Come in, Mrs Williams,' and he beckoned her away from the draughty door.

She stood there on one foot and held on to the lintels while her mouth moved as though in a search for words. It was no place for words.

Lewis John had flung himself free. He strode over to her, his eyes hard, fists clenched, and stood there before her in a gibber of rage.

'I must see you, Lewis,' she cried out, and made a frantic move towards him.

Then restraint went, like a taut cord bursting. He raised his clenched hands above him and then crashed them down on his head.

'Get out! GET OUT! Oh for Christ's sake . . . '

He flung his knotted fists towards her, as though to destroy the sight before him, and then ended in a hoarse moan. He stumbled back into the barn and brought a bare forearm across his wet brow, and sank slowly onto a bench.

Outside they could hear the short, hysterical crying and then that, too, had gone. And within no word: the shears had stopped, a sheep coughed, a bench creaked, a boot scraped over the slate floor. At last the old man's voice, like the gathered voice of all come in judgment:

'Lewis John Williams – you are falling very far short of what you . . . were.'

The lad lifted his head numbly under the chastisement and then lowered his eyes to the floor. He knew that, too. He wanted to tell himself, more than to tell them, that it was not true, that something had happened to him lately and he did not know what it was.

The old man's voice rose again.

'And we think better of you than *that*, my boy.'

'She has asked for it.'

The lad set his lips in a stolid, incommunicative way and stared before him.

'That is not the way to speak of your wife, either.'

The lad bowed his head under the reproach and the old man went on.

'There are certain things that are not said in

public – not said and not done, *whatever* the provocation.'

It was a point, granted the lad who lifted up his face in a dumb show of thanks.

'For your heart is in the right place, Lewis John, I will say that . . . ' The old man paid him this grudging tribute and then went on in a brighter voice, ' . . . and left to yourself there is no great harm in you.'

'No, indeed,' broke in Wili Owain, finding a place for himself. 'But as a man sows, Lewis *bach*. And Gwenna was the girl for you.'

Wili Owain wagged his head reassuringly in the cock-sure way of the knowing.

The lad winced as though cut to the quick. Wili Owain was a foolish man and was privileged to say foolish things so that he could not take him up.

But the others shuffled their feet uneasily and looked hard at the floor – that this of all things should have been said, and now of all times!

'Answer not a fool according to his folly,' broke in the old man in the same tranquil way, 'and there's no fool like the fool who means well. Come on, Lewis *bach*, we shall be friends yet.'

He got stiffly to his feet and slapped the lad across the shoulders. Lewis John looked up with the same harsh challenge, and then his better nature rose and took hold of him, his face gradually warmed into life again. He could not bear malice for long.

The old man groaned as he took a heavy ewe across his knee, and rubbed his hand over the timorous muzzle, looked into the sad, disdainful eyes with a comic, meditative squint.

'As a sheep before her shearers is dumb: and a damned good job too, boys *bach* – one old woman is enough in this life.'

And again the laughter rose, after how long an interval. It was like a thaw in a warm spring sun. The laughter and the native wit, the old stories told again, and a sudden burst of song as someone would take a bar or two out of sheer gladness of heart. And Lewis John threw himself heart and soul into it. It was the old life come back again. He made more droll the droll story and his laughing eye and the wild gleam of mischief in the young face provoked even the glum ones to extravagances. He and old John Shad were the natural leaders through whom all passed: and then they again, with the natural deference paid to each other's greatness, capped the other's sallies.

'Those were the days,' began Wili Owain, as though talking of a time gone. 'Remember, Lewis John, that night on the lake? Keepers all over the place and, *myn ufferni*, they had enough of it!'

Lewis John raised his head and looked out through the door to the broken, lifting sky over the mountain, and then he made a grimace as though the memory had come back like a known face to torment him. It was all too real. There was a lot about that night that no one would ever know – only he and Gwenna. There was no going back now, and he shook his head bitterly at the remembrance of something gone – the old life which, for all it may have been, was as real as the day itself.

'There's innocent for you!' someone taunted 'Have you ever seen a gaff, Lewis *bach*?'

'And the dog otter we killed on the way . . . '

Then old John Shad, raising his mildly browsing head:

'Was that the night that a young man climbed up a ladder to a lady's bedroom? Well, well! The keepers have been after me many a time, but there were never any ladders left lying about – though I was always in *hopes* . . . '

The laughter rose like a rustle around and he pulled at the white sweep of moustache with a sly, cocked eye.

' . . . because there are many cosier places than a night in gaol. No, boys *bach*, there were no ladders in my time, but oh dear me, a great deal of red flannel – and rough going it was: the path of true love was not as smooth as it might have been.'

There was no harsh voice now. Lewis John had entered into the life around him, just as though he had opened his hands and gathered it up. The sense of it was as real to him as something he saw and handled. He felt his spirit loosen within him like a hard knot in the belly gradually resolving itself. He gave himself in the same way, felt the touch of the sheep quicken in his hands, until his fingers no longer had a separate sense. The shears went surely, with a new rhythm as they sped over the warm flesh, and his eyes were alight with the felt joy of work.

That night was now so real that the actual physical sights and sounds came to him. He could smell the harsh tarn water in the rushes and raise his head to the taste of salt in the wind from the sea: the sour stink of sea birds that had made sodden the rush-clumps at the far-end, and the whiff of peat smoke somewhere far off.

He remembered that night – remembered plucking his cap off and turning his head up into the wind. The fading landscape was going in the way he knew: the deeper blood-red hue of mountains like a slow fuming fire in the thin light, and then a triumphant sky, with no longer a sun, far out over the sea. He remembered throwing his arms up, just in the exultation of being alive, then shaking his fists in defiance at something that he never, even now, understood. The wide, moving splendour overhead, the sense of a world so near that all the live sounds rose up in a last wailing cry in the stillness, and then so remote that the far-off, fading yellow sky over the sea was but a beginning.

All this came to him as he stood there. A day like all others, remembered by felt things – by wet earth and the chill of mountain water, and the soft pulp bellies of fish, felt under squeaking rushes: then the blue splendour of mountain and the fired sky far over the sea and a night coming, edged with frost and the blue sparkle of stars.

'*Duw* – that was a night!' He tossed his head up in the old triumphant way, the level white teeth showing in a grin and the wild gleam in his eyes like a light flashing.

Then, free of the sheep, he reached up to the rafters where some old gaffs lay on pegs, and made play with one. He got the haft bent under his forearm as he reached down to a fish, the body braced into a lean, poised curve and the eyes hard and lightless. And then he struck.

'Got him!' said old John Shad, looking up. 'Oh, he has not forgotten the way, whatever.'

Lewis John flung the gaff back with a gesture of disgust and sat down on the bench again. He pushed his hand up through the wet hair and screwed his eyes shut. Everything about that night had become too real.

The keepers had taken a hiding that time – one that they would long remember. And he, having fallen too far behind, had had to drop the salmon and swim the lake – right across to the Rectory on the far side where Gwenna worked. He had gone into the old church and carried the ladder from the broken bell-cote, through the rhododendron bushes to her window.

It was the end of a daft night. She tried to play off his fooling, as she had done so often before, when he would go off in a sulk, swearing that it was the end of all things. And yet she knew that a time would come when she would not have the strength to do so. She had known that almost as soon as she began to think about Lewis John at all, and she sought desperately to hide it from him in any way she could.

When at last he tried to clamber across the sill she shook her head with a slow, deliberate shake, not daring to trust her voice: but her unquiet, bounding heart and the lit-up eyes spoke for her.

And as he tried gently to unfasten her hands from across the window, she let her head droop downwards on her breast as the last act of surrender. And a look of dismay went, like a shadow, darkening her face, as she asked in an old, grave way:

'*I* know – but do you?'

As he carried her away from the window to the old cast iron bed of the maid's room, festooned with church texts, he tried out the solemn language of love (but with no great sureness), feeling that it was demanded of him.

'Gwenna – I'm . . . I'm awfully fond of you.'

'So it seems!'

The still grave face broke with the flash of a smile. And the wit was not lost on him. And for all that triumphant note that sounded in him he felt a long way behind, humbled by what she was.

Fused for ever in his own soul was that night. The two were one and indistinguishable: the riding triumph of the sky with its beckon into space, and Gwenna: the first brief bewilderment at life in the slowly widening eyes as passion woke, like a flower warmed out of the still earth. His own live world came back to him at the memory – so real that he felt he could reach out and touch it.

'*Duw* – what about a song, boys *bach?*'

He flung his head up in the old wild way. And then without more ado he broke into an old Welsh folk song. Its theme was the burden of young love, so old a song that their fathers had heard their grandfathers sing it at such another shearing, and yet as fresh now as ever. Young love and a sighing lover who in the dawn had followed the foot-tracks of the beloved one in the woodland hollows, so that he might kiss the pressure on the turf. Lewis John sang it very well. He breathed into it that fresh, pliant feeling the Welsh have, making it his own.

'Well done, well done,' chimed in old John Shad, brought up out of himself. They all applauded him. No one really believed it; Lewis John in the dawn, searching for the foot-prints of the cherished one on the woodland moss: but no one was meant to believe it. And at the same time they were to believe it, what had happened and what had not happened, the real and the unreal becoming one: the foolish, inconsequential lifting of the spirit which worked like leaven in the hard lump of life.

He took his place again and for a long time nothing more was said until, raising his head out of the sheep's belly as he let her go:

'*Duw* – what is the good of life if . . . if . . . '

'If what, *m'achgen'i?*'

John Shad was not listening: he had a fleece just coming loose at the neck and it needed care. He answered simply to show he had heard, and then bent his head still lower. Lewis John sat there, hands on his knees, head bowed.

'Last one for the morning!'

The old man straightened himself with a sigh. It was nearly time for the midday meal. And then, remembering something that had been said:

'What was that, *m'achgen'i?*'

'What is the good of . . . '

And then the words slowly faltered away. Gwenna stood at the door. She had a coarse sack apron round her; arms bare with the morning work were poised on the curving hips.

'Dinner, you men – and not so much singing,' she laughed in her mellow, lilting way.

She looked from one to another as though to ask whose had been the song. They stood back towards the wall in their discomfiture, eyes on the ground, leaving the lad alone before them.

'Oh – I see.'

She bit her lip until it seemed the blood would come and her eyes hardened like the cold gleam of steel. Then the colour surged like a loosened flood into her face, and beyond to her pounding breast.

They stood there for that one brief moment as though unable to free themselves one from the other. Then she turned with a wild toss of the head and ran on towards the house.

One by one the men had gone off in a stagger across the yard, stretching their cramped legs. They stopped at the stone spout and wrung their hands under the cold spring water and then flung them free. And then on towards the house, the high shrill laughter of women, the clatter of plates.

John Shad had stayed behind in the now empty barn. Once more he slipped his arm through the lad's in a final appeal.

'She must get *used* to seeing you, Lewis *bach*,' he pleaded.

Lewis John raised his head slowly from his knees as though he had heard for the first time.

'Ay – she shall, too!'

He nodded in the same grim, defiant way that she had had for him. Then he drew himself up and cocked his head with his old assurance. It was as if he had said that two could play at that game, and she should see . . .

But as he went across the yard the anger had already left him – there was only the tumult that welled up, like a hand clutched at the throat.

# For further reading

**Novels**
*Call Back Yesterday* (Jonathan Cape, 1935)
*The Heyday in the Blood* (Jonathan Cape, 1936)
*Watch for the Morning* (Jonathan Cape, 1938)
*Come Michaelmas* (Jonathan Cape, 1939)

**Short Stories**
*The White Farm and other stories* (Jonathan Cape, 1939)
*The Collected Stories of Geraint Goodwin*, ed. Roland Mathias and Sam Adams (H.G. Walters, 1976)

**Criticism**
Sam Adams, *Geraint Goodwin* in the *Writers of Wales* series (University of Wales Press, 1975)

# Images of Wales

The Corgi Series covers, no.18
*'The Gelding' by Sally Matthews (by kind permission of the artist)*

Sally Matthews, born in Tamworth in 1964, uses animals as a focus of aesthetic expression. She says, 'We can drive faster than a cheetah runs and kill quicker than a lion. We know how a horse moves and a bird flies. We may be amazed by *Wildlife on One*, but we forget, we do not live beside animals any more. Our admiration and the mystery of animals has been belittled by our achievement. We are not listening. They have senses and a reality that we have lost or never had.' Most of Sally Matthews' sculptures have been made outdoors in places such as Grizedale Forest, where their natural setting enhances their powerful effect.